"Good job s_nding those holiday gift baskets to  **praised, hi_ _____ _he ladies calle_ _____ _ing about how _____ _all thanks to you.**

"It's no biggie, Max. I was just doing my job."

"No, as usual, you went above and beyond the call of duty, and it's greatly appreciated. You're a godsend, Jada. I don't know what I'd do without you."

Jada returned his smile, taking a moment to admire his chiseled facial features and his stylish gray suit. A self-proclaimed ladies' man with a penchant for European models, Max was working his way through the lingerie catalog roster, and often joked about eloping with a centerfold. Every time he did, Jada felt a profound sense of sadness. Max was everything her father had warned her to stay away from, but it didn't stop Jada from crushing on her dreamy boss. Jada was attracted to scholarly types, men who loved to discuss literature and world history, but everything about Max appealed to her—his lopsided grin, his devil-may-care attitude, the thousand-dollar Cuban cigars he smoked in his office at the end of the workday—and over the years her feelings for him had grown.

Dear Reader,

Have you ever had a crush on someone but was scared to tell them the truth? Was it your boss? That's the predicament Jada Allen finds herself in in *A Los Angeles Rendezvous*. They come from two different worlds—Maximillian "Max" Moore was raised in the lap of luxury and Jada's from the wrong side of the tracks—but Jada can't help but desire her sinfully sexy boss with the devilish grin. And when Max kisses her at the office Christmas party, Jada wonders if her dreams have finally come true.

Max has a lot on his plate. He's at odds with Taylor (his feisty ten-year-old daughter), his ex-wife hates him, his business rival is gunning for him and his dad is battling a terminal illness. Thank God he can rely on Jada. After Jada gets a sizzling holiday makeover, Max sees his administrative assistant in a new light. A romantic weekend in Maui sets his heart—and his libido—on fire, and Max sets out to prove to Jada he is worthy of her love.

If you enjoyed the Millionaire Moguls series, spread the word and connect with me at pamelayaye@aol.com, or on my social media pages.

All the best in life and love,

Pamela Yaye

A
LOS ANGELES
RENDEZVOUS

PAMELA
YAYE

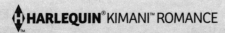

HARLEQUIN® KIMANI™ ROMANCE

Special thanks and acknowledgment are given to Pamela Yaye
for her contribution to the Millionaire Moguls series.

Recycling programs
for this product may
not exist in your area.

ISBN-13: 978-1-335-21695-3

A Los Angeles Rendezvous

Copyright © 2018 by Harlequin Books S.A.

Printed in U.S.A.

Pamela Yaye has a bachelor's degree in Christian education. Her love for African American fiction prompted her to pursue a career in writing romance. When she's not working on her latest novel, this busy wife, mother and teacher is watching basketball, cooking or planning her next vacation. Pamela lives in Alberta, Canada, with her gorgeous husband and adorable, but mischievous, son and daughter.

Books by Pamela Yaye

Harlequin Kimani Romance

Seduced by the Playboy
Seduced by the CEO
Seduced by the Heir
Seduced by Mr. Right
Heat of Passion
Seduced by the Hero
Seduced by the Mogul
Mocha Pleasures
Seduced by the Bachelor
Secret Miami Nights
Seduced by the Tycoon at Christmas
Pleasure in His Kiss

Visit the Author Profile page
at Harlequin.com for more titles.

Chapter 1

"Good afternoon, Millennium Talent Agency," Jada Allen chirped, pressing the headset closer to her ear so she could hear the caller over the noise in the reception area. She'd worked at the agency for two years, as an administrative assistant to Maximillian "Max" Moore—one of the most successful Hollywood talent agents in the business—and the only thing the twenty-seven-year-old Inglewood native loved more than her job was cheesecake. "How may I help you?"

"Is Max in? I've been texting him all day, but he hasn't responded, and I'm worried…"

Jada recognized the high-pitched voice with the Spanish accent. She couldn't believe the actress was calling again—the third time in thirty minutes. Max didn't want a serious relationship with the Mexican beauty, and had broken things off with the TV sitcom star days earlier. Jada should know. She'd sent the "breakup" flowers to the actress's Beverly Hills condo, with a Hallmark card, but every time the brunette called the office she sounded more upset, almost hysterical. Jada adored Max and was proud to be his assistant, but his favorite hobby seemed to be breaking hearts, and she worried one day he'd mess with the wrong woman and pay the price.

A chilling thought came to mind. What if the Mexican beauty came after Max? Sought revenge? What if he got hurt? Max was all about the chase, but once he slept with the object of his affection he lost interest, every single time. Jada only hoped his womanizing ways wouldn't get him in trouble.

"I need to talk to him… It's important…"

"I'm sorry, but Mr. Moore isn't available right now. He stepped out," Jada lied. The truth was, Max was in his office, alone, but Jada didn't want the actress to show up at the agency unannounced and cause a scene.

"Tell him Josefina Acosta called. I need to speak to him ASAP. It's an emergency…"

It always is, Jada thought, adjusting her oval-shaped eyeglasses. Hanging up, she turned back to her computer screen. Logging on to the internet, she checked the Outlook calendar for Monday's meeting, appointments and conference calls. Jada made a mental note to confirm Max's travel plans for his business trip to New York before she left for the day.

The desk phone rang. A female was on the line, demanding to speak to Max, but Jada took a message and hung up. All day, she'd been fielding phone calls from women who were eager to speak to Max, but it didn't surprise her. It was Friday, and his "girlfriends" were busy making plans for the weekend. They wanted to spend their free time with him, and it was evident by

the desperation in their voices that they were willing
to do anything to make it happen.

Of course they were desperate for him. Everyone
was—including Jada. It was hard to find something
about him she didn't like. Max was the kind of man
people gravitated toward and instantly hit it off with.
Charismatic and drop-dead handsome, he had dozens
of A-list clients, knew everyone who mattered in LA
and was invited to the hottest parties in town. He was
a well-known, highly respected agent, who negotiated
multimillion-dollar contracts for his clients. And not
only did Max have a remarkable eye for talent, he had a
knack for pitching ideas to television and movie executives. Was so good at it he had a production deal with
an LA studio. Max pushed himself to be the best, and
everyone who mattered thought he was.

For the second time in minutes, Jada admired the
framed photographs hanging on the vibrant blue walls
in the reception area. In every picture, the twenty-eight-
year-old talent agent looked confident, and was grinning
from ear to ear. Max lived for his work. He schmoozed.
He networked. He wheeled and dealed. He charmed and
seduced. He was known for being a ruthless negotia-
tor, and his keen deal-making skills had helped make
him—and his clients—filthy rich. Millennium Talent
Agency was a prestigious boutique agency, and the business awards prominently displayed on the glass shelf
proved how hard Max worked.

Jada picked up her mug and tasted her peppermint
tea. It was her favorite time of year, and everything about
the holiday season made her smile. Christmas was several weeks away, and Jada was looking forward to the
holiday festivities in LA. There was the Christmas Ball
at the Sheraton Hotel, Cocktails under the Mistletoe at

a popular jazz lounge in Santa Monica and several exclusive Prescott George events, as well. Prescott George was a national organization for African-American millionaires, founded in the 1940s, and Max was a proud, card-carrying member. The club was as discreet as it was powerful; members couldn't buy their way in—they had to be invited. The Moguls were more than just wealthy businessmen with yachts, mansions and private planes: they did good work. For decades, they'd provided college scholarships to needy students, funding to inner-city organizations and million-dollar donations to local charities. Every year, Max invited his staff to the Prescott George charity bash on Christmas Eve, and Jada wouldn't miss the celebrity-filled party for anything in the world.

Jada's ears perked up. Leaning forward in her chair, she listened to the college interns as they strode through the lobby, praising the chic holiday decor throughout the main floor. Beaming, she watched the trio snap selfies in front of the ten-foot evergreen tree positioned in the corner of the room. To make the reception area look festive, she'd hung up velvet stockings and mistletoe around the room, sprinkled garland on the leafy potted plants and taped oversize red ribbons to the windows. All week, several female staff had tried to get Max under the mistletoe, but he was always on the move and would rather hang out in his office, making calls and reading scripts, than in the reception area.

"I asked you to make me look good, and you delivered…"

Peppermint tea sloshed over the side of Jada's mug and splashed onto her gray pencil skirt, creating a damp spot. At the sound of Max's voice, lust filled her body. His silky-smooth baritone was the sexiest thing her ears had ever heard, and when Jada glanced away from her computer screen and spotted Max standing in the doorway of his office, her mouth watered. Her boss was one of the most eligible and desirable bachelors in LA, and for good reason. Six feet tall, with buttery brown skin, soulful eyes and a body that was pure perfection, he was every woman's dream. If Hollywood had a Sexiest Man award, Max Moore would win it every year. Jada had been working for the UCLA graduate for years, but every time he looked at her she felt light-headed, out of it, as if she suddenly had no control over her body.

It was a miracle he even hired me, she thought, cringing at the memory that flashed in her mind. She'd been so nervous during their thirty-minute interview that she'd stuttered and stumbled over her words. If not for her stellar résumé and references, Max probably would have shown her the door, and she would have missed out on working at the popular talent agency. Located only a few blocks from the iconic Kodak Theater on a busy, tree-lined street, Millennium Talent Agency was filled with plush furniture, exotic plants, contemporary artwork and a marble wet bar. Sophisticated and überposh, the office had a tranquil ambience, and Jada made sure everyone who walked through the front doors—whether it was an aspiring actress, a D-list actor or an up-and-coming boy band—received VIP service.

"Good job sending those personalized gift baskets to Brielle and Felicity," Max praised, his voice filled with awe. "Both ladies called me this afternoon, gushing about how sweet and thoughtful I am, and it's all thanks to you."

"It's no biggie, Max. I was just doing my job."

"No, as usual, you went above and beyond the call

of duty, and it's greatly appreciated. You're a godsend, Jada. I don't know what I'd do without you."

Jada returned his smile. She took a moment to admire his chiseled facial features and his stylish gray suit. A self-proclaimed ladies' man with a penchant for European models, Max was working his way through the Victoria's Secret catalog, and often joked about eloping with a centerfold. Every time he did, Jada felt a profound sense of sadness. Max was the kind of guy her father had warned her to stay away from, but Jada couldn't stop crushing on her dreamy boss. She was attracted to scholarly types, men who loved to discuss literature and world history, but everything about Max appealed to her—his lopsided grin, his devil-may-care attitude, the thousand-dollar Cuban cigars he smoked in his office at the end of the workday—and over the years her feelings for him had grown.

"You're leaving?" she asked, noticing the brown leather satchel he was holding in his right hand. "Another hot date with *Sports Illustrated*'s Swimsuit Model of the Year?"

"I wish. Nothing beats spending the night with a beautiful, curvaceous woman."

He flashed a wicked grin, and desire rippled across Jada's flesh. Dimples pinched his cheeks, and if that wasn't bad enough, he smelled of expensive cologne, a scent that was so strong and masculine it was wreaking havoc on her body. Then Max licked his lips and a tingle shot down her spine. The moment she'd laid eyes on him it had been lust at first sight, and over the years nothing had changed. It was hard to find something about Max she didn't like, and despite his womanizing ways, Jada still wanted him. She couldn't imagine a better Christmas gift than making love to the eligible bachelor from Santa Monica with the killer physique.

"I'm going to visit my dad at his estate," he explained. "My brothers called an emergency family meeting tonight, so I canceled my business dinner with Big Ticket Movies executives and rescheduled it for first thing Monday morning."

Jada wore a sympathetic expression on her face. "How is Reginald doing?"

"As well as can be expected. Despite his prognosis, he's in good spirits."

"That's great, Max. I'm glad to hear that. Is he doing chemotherapy?"

"No, he can't..." His voice broke, and seconds passed before he could finish his sentence. "It's too late. His doctors said it won't help, and suggested he get his will in order."

The phone buzzed in her headset, cuing Jada she had an incoming call, but she ignored it. Wanted Max to know she cared about him, and his family. Standing, Jada took off her headset, dropped it on the desk and approached him.

"Dr. Petrov said there isn't anything more they can do for him, but I'm not giving up hope. Hope is all I have left."

Jada smiled sadly. Five years ago, his mother had died from cancer, and now his father was battling the debilitating disease. Despite everything happening in his personal life, Max hadn't lost his sense of humor and was always joking around with his staff in the break room. But yesterday, when Jada walked into his office with the day's mail, she'd found him sitting behind his executive desk with tears streaming down his cheeks. He'd laughed it off, saying he had something in his eyes, but Jada didn't believe him. Knew he was lying. She'd seen the anguished expression on his face, sensed his pain and couldn't resist giving him a hug. Holding Max in her arms had been amazing, and now Jada felt closer to him than ever before. "I can't imagine what you're going through, Max, but I'm here for you. Anything you need. Just ask, and it's done."

"Thanks, Jada. It's great knowing I can always count on you."

I wish I could do more. Like kiss you—

"Hey, did you check out that vlog I sent you?"

Jada cleared her mind. "Yeah, but I didn't think Kid Quentin was funny. Sorry."

"Are you kidding me? His celebrity impersonations are spot-on, his comedic timing is remarkable, and I almost died laughing when he flipped his skateboard in front of Times Square and chipped his front tooth." His face lit up as he chuckled, and his mood seemed to brighten. "Mark my words—the kid's going to be a famous child star!"

"I believe you," Jada said, fervently nodding her head. "You're the one with the eye for talent, Max, not me. I'm just your lowly assistant."

Max spoke in a stern tone of voice. "Don't talk like that. You're not a lowly assistant. You're my right-hand girl…"

Her breath caught in her throat, and for the first time in Jada's life she was speechless. Every morning, when she arrived at the office at seven o'clock, Max was already hard at work in his office, answering emails, reading contracts and scheduling meetings, so his words surprised her. Made her head spin and her skin warm. *Max thinks I'm special? I'm important to him? I'm the best administrative assistant he's ever had?*

Jada resisted the urge to dance around the room. Pride filled her and made her heart light. A smile teased her lips. *Not bad for a girl from Inglewood*, Jada thought, as bitter memories of her childhood overwhelmed her mind. Her parents, Colette and Ezekiel Allen, had split up after fifteen years of marriage, and when her mom had relocated to New York to chase her dreams of stardom on Broadway, custody of Jada and her three younger siblings had been awarded to her dad. Money had been tight, and juggling three custodian jobs left Ezekiel little time for his children, so Jada had picked up the slack in his absence. Now her family was thriving and closer than ever. Jada talked to her mom several times a year, and that was more than enough. They weren't close, and she didn't miss her. As a child, she'd always feared her mother's temper and found solace in her dad's arms. Ezekiel had been her mother *and* father, and Jada loved him dearly.

"I better get going. I have to pick up Taylor by six o'clock, or my ex will kill me."

"Wow, two weekends in a row with your beautiful daughter. That's awesome!" she exclaimed.

"Taylor's grandmother, Shay's mom, had surgery, and she'll need a lot of help once she's discharged, so I offered to take Taylor for the weekend." He shrugged a shoulder. "It was the right thing to do."

"You're a great dad, Max."

"Tell that to Taylor. She hates me!"

Jada scoffed. "No, she doesn't. Don't say that."

"It's the craziest thing. I can manage the careers of dozens of clients, but I can't manage a successful relationship with my ten-year-old daughter. If we're butting heads now, what's life going to be like when she's sixteen?" Max shivered. "It's a chilling thought."

"Taylor's going through a phase. Don't sweat it. It's perfectly normal, Max."

"I hope so, but I still wish she was my sweet little girl who used to think the world of me." Releasing a deep sigh, he retrieved his iPhone from his jacket pocket and swiped a finger across the screen. "Have a good weekend, Jada. See you on Monday."

Max put on his sunglasses and marched through the front door, whistling a tune.

Slumping against the desk, Jada fanned her face. Her attraction to Max was so powerful and intense she needed a moment to catch her breath. Her mouth was wet and her pulse pounded in her ears, making it impossible for her to think straight. She had memos to write and emails to answer, but Jada couldn't stop fantasizing about Max and all the delicious things she'd like to do to him—on his expensive executive desk.

Chapter 2

Max strode into the lavish great room of his childhood home in Malibu, took one look at his ailing father sitting on the couch and willed the tears in his eyes not to fall. Reginald used to be a tall, imposing figure with a toothy grin and dynamic personality, but now he was a shadow of his former self. His reputation destroyed after the scandal in San Diego and his longtime friends casting him aside, he found little these days to be cheerful about, and Max missed his father's hearty laughter. Reginald's membership in Prescott George—one of his greatest pleasures in his life—was revoked because an internal investigation had uncovered solid evidence against him in the sabotage case. Less than a week later, he'd received devastating news. He was diagnosed with stage four prostate cancer and his doctors didn't think he'd live past the New Year. No one did, but Max was holding out hope for a Christmas miracle and believed with all his heart that Reginald would beat the odds. If anyone could, it was his gutsy fifty-nine-year-old dad.

Life is so unfair. Why me? Why my family? Max thought, taking off his sunglasses and dropping them on the coffee table covered in business magazines. *First my mom gets cancer, and now my dad. Haven't I suffered enough?* Burying his pain, he marched confidently through the living room toward his dad, sporting a smile.

Bathed in natural light, the mansion had a chef's kitchen, an in-home movie theater, an art studio and three master bedrooms. The glass walls provided picturesque views of the lush green landscape, but the tranquil scenery did nothing to soothe Max's troubled mind.

The mansion held great memories for Max, and seeing his mother's oil paintings displayed on the fireplace mantel made sadness prick his heart. Constance Moore hadn't been just his mom; she'd been his best friend. She'd quit her high-powered managerial job at the Getty Center to raise him and his older stepsister, Bianca, and when his mom wasn't volunteering at their private school or baking cookies for his soccer team, she was chauffeuring him around to his extracurricular activities. Growing up, his friends had loved coming to his house, and Constance was the reason why. She had a warm, caring nature and made everyone who visited their home feel welcome. Not a day went by that Max didn't think about his mom, and his only regret in life was that he hadn't been at her bedside when she took her last breath.

"What's up, fam?" Max greeted his half brothers with a fist bump. Lean, with close-cropped hair, intense eyes and stylish designer eyeglasses, Trey looked more like an actor than a Hollywood screenwriter at the top of his game. He'd fallen hard for Kiara Woods, the owner of *the* preschool for the children of Hollywood's elite, and stunned everyone who knew him when he'd proposed. She'd said yes, and the couple was busy planning their spring wedding.

"I thought you'd never get here. What took you so long?" Derek asked, glancing at his gold wristwatch. Tall, toned and athletic, Derek was a successful real-estate mogul who collected properties the way rap stars collected luxury cars. Last month, he'd reconnected with his first love, model Alexis Armstrong, and after a passionate night together they'd discovered they were pregnant. He'd popped the question on Thanksgiving Day, and the parents-to-be were overjoyed about the impending birth of their child and their upcoming fairy-tale wedding.

Max had never been close to his brothers, but they'd been working together for weeks to clear Reginald's name, and now he respected and admired them. "It's good to see you, Dad. How are things?"

"Can't complain. Had a massage this afternoon, and Tanesha sang my favorite Christmas song. It was amazing. Hours later, I can still hear her angelic voice in my ears." Closing his eyes, he snapped his fingers and hummed a tune. "You should sign her to your agency, son. She's talented, and cute as a button."

Max nodded as his dad spoke, even though he had no intention of meeting the singing masseuse from Brentwood.

Observing his dad, Max found it hard to believe Reginald used to be two hundred pounds of steel-hard muscle. He was thin and frail now, the disease having ravaged his body. It took everything in Max not to cry as he stared at his dad. He couldn't imagine his life without him and struggled to control his emotions. Without Reginald, his life would be empty, and it pained him that Taylor wouldn't have any more Sunday afternoon "dates" with her grandfather. He'd never take her for ice cream again, or teach her how to play spades, or how to drive a stick shift.

"Son, if you sign her to your talent agency, do I get a finder's fee?" Reginald joked, arching an eyebrow. "I think fifty percent is fair. After all, *I* discovered her."

Max wore a wry smile, chuckling when his dad called him a cheapskate. In spite of everything Reginald had been through—his wife's sudden death, losing his membership to Prescott George, the groundless accusations against him and his heartbreaking diagnosis—he'd never lost his smile, and it gave Max hope, the strength to get out of bed and face the world every day even though he was broken inside.

"I hate to interrupt this touching Hallmark moment, but we need to discuss Demetrius."

There was a note of bitterness in Derek's tone, but Max didn't say anything. Wisely held his tongue. He didn't want to argue with his brother in front of Reginald. That was the last thing their father needed, and Max didn't want to say or do anything to stress him out. "What about him? Did you uncover more information linking Demetrius to the sabotage case? Are we any closer to clearing Dad's name?"

"No, not yet, but I'm working hard on it."

"Then what's on your mind, D? Why do you look so stressed?"

"Because nothing makes sense," he complained. "Why would Demetrius want to frame you? You've been his oldest and dearest friend for decades."

Reginald dropped his gaze to his lap. "I, ah, have no idea."

"Of course you do," Trey snapped, his tone matter-of-fact. "You're not fooling anyone, Dad. It's obvious you're lying, and it's time to come clean."

His brothers grilled Reginald until sweat dripped from his brow.

"Why are you blaming me? What makes you think I did something wrong?"

"Because before you got kicked out of Prescott George, you were a jerk," Derek said. "You didn't think of anyone but yourself, and it was infuriating."

"It's true, I was, but I've changed for the better."

Derek and Trey shared a "Yeah, right" look, and Max knew they didn't believe their father. Was this why his brothers had called an emergency family meeting? Because they wanted him to grill Reginald? Well, it wasn't going to happen. His brothers always made him feel guilty for having a close relationship with their father, but he wasn't going to stand by and let them bash Reginald. Not now. Their dad was sick, physically and emotionally spent, and Max didn't want his brothers ganging up on him. No one truly understood what Reginald was going through, and he wanted him to feel supported, not insulted. "Guys, ease up. Dad's had a rough few weeks, so quit badgering him about Demetrius. He'll confide in us when he's ready."

"How long are we supposed to wait? Time is of the essence," Trey pointed out. "Dad, if you want us to help you, you have to be honest with us about everything."

"We'll never get to the bottom of things if you keep coddling him," Derek said, addressing Max, his gaze dark and narrowed. "Reginald needs to be straight up with us, so we can clear his name and put this mess behind us."

Reginald coughed into his fist. "I... I—I can't. I don't want you boys to think less of me."

Derek scoffed. "Too late for *that*. We know who you are and what you're capable of, and to be honest, there's nothing you can say or do to surprise me..."

Derek trailed off when Max silenced him with a look. Reginald wasn't perfect; he'd screwed up and made mistakes—mistakes Trey and Derek liked throwing in his face over and over again. His brothers hadn't grown up with Reginald, but Max had a very different relationship with his father and saw him as a loving, loyal family man. When Reginald was married to Trey's mother, he'd cheated on her with Derek's mother, refused to acknowledge Derek as his kid until a court-ordered DNA test proved it, then found his soul mate in Max's mother. Reginald was so in love with Constance that he'd never had another adulterous affair and had remained faithful until her death. It saddened him that his brothers had such a negative opinion of Reginald. He'd been a father to Max in every sense of the word, and he had enough memories of his dad to fill a hundred scrapbooks. Reginald had taught him to ride a bike, taken him to his first NBA game, and attended his school events, even if it meant leaving work early. "'He who's without sin cast the first stone,'" Max said, quoting the well-known Bible verse. "Dad isn't perfect, and neither are you. Hell, no one is, so cut him some slack, would ya?"

Derek took his car keys out of his pocket. "This is a waste of time. I'm out of here."

"Me, too." Trey got up. "Dad, when you're ready to have an honest conversation about your past and explain the real reason behind your beef with Demetrius, let me know."

Trey and Derek strode through the great room, speaking in hushed tones.

"I slept with Ellen," Reginald blurted out.

Trey and Derek stopped and turned. All three men faced their dad, eyes wide, jaws slack. They'd asked him outright a couple weeks ago if he'd had an affair with Demetrius's wife, and Reginald had denied it.

"You did what?" Derek shouted.

Max cursed. He couldn't wrap his head around his father's confession. All this time, he'd thought that his dad was grieving the loss of his mom, so he was shocked to hear about his father's tryst with Demetrius Davis's former trophy wife, Ellen Davis. "Dad, how could you? Demetrius is your best friend, and he's always been like a second father to us."

Trey closed his gaping mouth. "Are you insane? What were you thinking?"

"I-i-it was an accident," Reginald stammered, in a shaky voice.

Throwing his hands in the air, Derek rolled his eyes to the ceiling. "An accident? How do you accidentally sleep with your best friend's wife? Explain that to me. I'm dying to know."

"I was lonely, and she was upset about Demetrius neglecting her and came on to me one afternoon when I stopped by the house. It only happened once. I swear on my life."

Only once? Yeah, right, Dad, and I'm a born-again virgin! Max knew Reginald was lying, but didn't expose him. It would only make things worse, and he didn't want his brothers to go off on their dad. He remembered seeing Reginald and Ellen at an expensive

French restaurant last summer, but Max had been at a business meeting and never had an opportunity to speak to them. And old friends of Reginald and Demetrius had also mentioned seeing the pair together a few times. Wow, they'd had an affair? Demetrius must have found out about it and thought he could kill two birds with one stone: hurt the San Diego chapter's chances of winning Chapter of the Year *and* frame his "best friend" as payback.

Max didn't want to believe it, felt guilty for even thinking such a horrible thing about the successful businessman, but the truth was staring him in the face.

"No wonder Demetrius hates you," Trey said, shaking his head. "You're lucky he didn't strangle you for messing with his wife. I would."

"I don't understand how he found out. No one knew about our affair. Unless..." Reginald straightened in his seat. "It had to be Ellen. She promised to take our secret to the grave, but threw me under the bus. I can't believe this shit."

Max shrugged. "Never trust a big butt and a smile."

Reginald chuckled so hard his shoulders shook. Max felt a rush of pride. It had been weeks since he'd heard his father's hearty laugh, and the sound was music to his ears. As he thought about Reginald's shocking confession, Max weighed his options. He didn't want to make waves in Prescott George, but he had to act. Had to prove to everyone in the organization that his dad wasn't the cunning, conniving snake Demetrius said he was.

Guilt tormented his conscience. It killed Max that Demetrius had framed his dad. But everything pointed to it. Which made Max feel even worse: his father had been telling the truth all along, but he'd doubted him. The evidence had been indisputable—until it wasn't.

But no one had believed Reginald. Because his father hadn't lived an upstanding life, Prescott George members had rushed to judgment. Deep down, Max had had a hard time believing Reginald had done the things he'd been accused of, but he'd sided with the organization instead of standing by his father, and his earlier position filled him with remorse.

Max rested his hands on his dad's shoulders, wanted him to feel loved and supported. Now that he knew why Demetrius hated Reginald, he could finally clear his dad's name. And he would. By any means necessary. Even if it meant raising hell. No one messed with his family and got away with it—not even a man he used to admire. Demetrius was going down, and when Trey and Derek nodded their heads, Max knew they shared the same thought.

Chapter 3

Max parked his orange Ferrari 458 on the driveway of his ex-wife's Tudor-style home, jumped out of the car and activated the alarm. Still reeling from what Reginald had said at the family meeting, Max struggled to put one foot in front of the other. He couldn't stop thinking about the sabotage case, or the heartless things Demetrius had done to his father.

Glancing down at his cell phone, he wondered if it was too late to call Jada at the office. He wanted to vent about his frustrations and knew she'd understand what he was going through. She always did. The truth was, Jada knew him better than anyone—even his siblings—and he trusted her explicitly. Petite, with a soft voice and shy demeanor, she was so darn likable everyone in the office adored her. At times, Jada got flustered when one of his male clients flirted with her, but she had a dazzling smile and the cutest laugh he'd ever heard. She was wise beyond her years, and Max valued her opinion. Most important, Jada wasn't afraid to disagree with him, or tell it like it was, especially when it came to his daughter, and he loved her for it.

To clear his mind, Max took a deep breath. He had to get a hold of himself, had to stop fretting about his problems. He was spending the weekend with Taylor, and he didn't want her to know he was upset. His daughter was ten years old, but these days it seemed as if she was speaking a different language. Even though Max saw his daughter for dinner three times a week, they barely communicated. Lately, everything he said and did was wrong. They used to be close, used to laugh and joke around, but ever since Taylor turned ten it had been hard to connect with her.

Before Max could ring the buzzer the front door opened, and Shay appeared with a scowl on her face and a hand on her hip. Even though she was glaring at him, she looked youthful and pretty in a striped off-the-shoulder sweater, skinny jeans and suede boots.

"Hey, Shay. How are things?"

"Max, what are you doing here? You're supposed to pick up Taylor tomorrow."

"No," he corrected her, shaking his head to underscore his point. "On Monday we agreed that I'd come get her today after work, so here I am."

"Oh, really? It must have slipped my empty little mind." Leaning against the door frame, Shay folded her arms across her chest and rolled her eyes skyward. "*Or* you changed the plans at the last minute, which you have a habit of doing whenever it suits you."

Max said nothing, knew if he did they'd end up arguing, and he didn't want to butt heads with his ex-wife. They'd been divorced for years, but nothing had changed: Shay still looked at him with disgust, as if she couldn't stand to be in his presence, and it annoyed the hell out of him. He'd never been "Husband of the Year," but he'd been a great provider, and because of his tenacity, hard work and ambition—and his generous alimony payments—she could afford to live in the most desirable neighborhood in Santa Monica.

How had things gone so bad so quick? Max wondered for the umpteenth time. He'd met Shay Wilcox his freshman year of high school and fallen hard for the voluptuous student-body president. To his shock and amazement, they'd gotten pregnant on prom night despite using a condom. Max, who'd been raised in a happy home with two parents who were madly in love, proposed, figuring they'd repeat his parents' success, even though they were teenagers. But by the time Taylor was born they were bickering nonstop. Max thought providing a great life for his family was everything. Being a workaholic had caused a rift between him and Shay; he was so busy going to university, trying to be a good father to their daughter and interning at a hot new talent agency that he was neglecting his wife without even realizing it. Shay had wanted a more hands-on partner instead of a husband who was always on the phone—making deals, soothing upset clients, and reading contracts and movie scripts at the dinner table. Being young parents took its toll on their relationship and it didn't survive, despite them both trying hard to make things work. After seven years of marriage, Shay had filed for divorce, and now Max's focus was on keeping the peace in his family and improving his relationship with Taylor.

"How is your mother feeling? Has she finally been discharged from the hospital?"

"Don't worry about my mom. She's fine."

Fine? Really? But she had major surgery yesterday! It was obvious Shay didn't want to talk to him about her mother's health, or anything else, so Max peered inside the house in search of his spunky daughter. "Can you let Taylor know I'm here?"

Shay gestured to the gate with a nod of her head, and her ponytail swished back and forth. "Taylor's in the backyard with her friends. Good luck getting her to leave."

"I'm her dad. Of course she'll want to go with me. I have big plans for us tonight."

"If you say so," Shay quipped, wearing a doubtful expression on her face. "See ya!"

Hearing his cell phone ring, Max took it out of his back pocket and read his newest text message. Strolling along the stone walkway, he could hear singing and laughing, and knew his daughter was having the time of her life with the neighborhood kids. For a moment, he considered leaving so she could hang out with her friends, but changed his mind. How were things supposed to get better if they didn't spend quality time together? If he didn't show Taylor that he loved her and valued their father-daughter weekends? These days, Max couldn't seem to connect with her, but he wasn't going to give up.

Max opened the gate, spotted Taylor in the outdoor living room with her friends and froze like one of the marble statues decorating the flower garden. An upbeat pop song was playing on the stereo system, but his daughter was slow-dancing with a tall, lanky boy who wore an Adidas sweat suit and sported a Mohawk hairstyle. Max couldn't believe his eyes.

Gazing up at her dance partner, Taylor draped her arms around the boy's scrawny neck.

His jaw dropped. Max wanted to pummel the kid in the ground when he kissed Taylor on the cheek, but exercised self-control. *Good God! Is Taylor wearing makeup?* Scrutinizing her appearance, Max cursed under his breath. Her cheeks were rosy, and her lips were glossy and pink. Diamond stud earrings twinkled in her ears, colorful bracelets filled her arms, and long, thin braids hung loosely over her shoulders. Taylor looked adorable in her Zendaya-themed sweatshirt, leggings and high-top gold sneakers, and his anger abated when he noticed she was wearing the heart-shaped silver necklace he'd bought her weeks earlier at the mall.

"What's going on here?" Max shouted, jogging across the manicured grass.

Taylor dropped her hands to her sides and stepped away from her dance partner. "Dad, what are you doing here? Shouldn't you be at work?"

"Say goodbye to your friends," Max said. "You're spending the weekend with me, so go inside and grab your stuff. You have five minutes."

Her face fell, and her shoulders sagged. "But I want to stay here. Do I have to?"

Max felt a twinge of disappointment, but he smiled. He didn't want Taylor or her friends to know that her response hurt his feelings. There was a time when he couldn't go anywhere without Taylor nipping at his heels, and it saddened him that his only daughter would rather hang out with her friends than have a father-daughter date with him. "I have a fun weekend planned for us, and I know you're going to love it, so let's get out of here."

"Where are we going?"

"That's for me to know and for you to find out."

Giving Taylor a one-arm hug, he kissed her forehead. He didn't care that her friends were watching them. He wanted his daughter to know that she was special to him, and that nothing mattered more to him than making her smile. "I will say this. There's a butt-kicking at Monster Mini Golf with your name on it, and I can't *wait* to beat you! You're going down, Taylor Moore."

"Okay, okay, I'm coming. Let me just say 'bye to my friends. I'll meet you out front."

Marching back through the yard, Max unbuttoned his suit jacket and loosened the knot in his tie. He couldn't help wondering what would have happened if he hadn't shown up when he did, and made a mental note to speak to Shay about supervising Taylor and her friends outside.

Minutes later, Taylor opened the passenger-side door of the Ferrari, clutching her purple backpack in one hand and her shiny gold iPod in the other. Sunshine rained down on them through the open sunroof, and the cool evening breeze flooded the car with a refreshing scent. "Ready to go down?" Max put on his seat belt.

"Ha! Dad, you couldn't beat me at mini golf if I was blindfolded!"

It felt good joking around with Taylor, made Max feel as if he'd done something right, for once. Cruising down the street, he noticed teenagers playing basketball, joggers breezing through the park and moms pushing designer baby strollers.

"Looks like *someone* loves her new iPod," Max said, gesturing to the electronic device in his daughter's hands. To make her laugh, he wiggled his eyebrows, then winked. Taylor giggled, and the sound brought a wide smile to his lips.

"I don't like it. I *love* it! It's the best birthday present

I've ever gotten, and my friends are totally jealous that I have the newest version." Taylor plugged the device into the Bluetooth system, selected the song she wanted to hear and faced him, her eyes round and bright. "Can you set the date and the time on my iPod? I tried to do it last night, Mom, too, but we couldn't do it."

"I don't know anything about iPods. I'll call Jada. She'll help us—"

Taylor bolted upright in her seat, as if she'd been pricked with a pin, and Max broke off speaking.

"What's wrong?"

"Y-y-you didn't buy my iPod?" she stammered.

Shame burned his cheeks, and perspiration wet his pin-striped dress shirt. "Taylor, honey, I'm sorry. I didn't mean to upset you," he said, patting her leg. "Jada bought your birthday present because I asked her to. I knew you'd love it, and I was right."

"What about the card? And all the nice things you wrote about me? You said the day I was born was the happiest day of your life, and that being my dad was your greatest joy…"

Max coughed to clear the lump in his throat. *Oh, snap! I shouldn't have said anything about Jada's involvement!* Damn. He'd messed up. Now Taylor's lips were pursed, her arms were folded across her chest, and she was glaring at him with more intensity than Shay did. It was at times like these that Max wished he could hit the rewind button and cram the words back into his mouth. Of course, Jada had bought the iPod and loaded it with his daughter's favorite music. His assistant always picked the right thing; it was why she was his right-hand woman. His best employee. Jada chose all the gifts for the people in his life, including Taylor, his girlfriends and his celebrity clients. Not to mention she made everything run smoothly at the office and went above and beyond her job description.

"Did you write the note inside my birthday card, or did Ms. Jada do it for you?"

His mouth was so dry he couldn't speak.

"I should have known you didn't buy it," Taylor said, staring out the windshield. "You're too busy working twelve-hour days and chasing thots to do anything nice for me."

Staring at Taylor in disbelief, Max gripped the steering wheel so hard his knuckles cracked. Did his tween daughter just say what he *thought* she said? He was glad they were stopped at the intersection, because if he'd been driving he probably would have driven off the road and crashed into a palm tree. Her words stung, and he didn't appreciate her tone. Taylor sounded like Shay— cold, bitter and angry—and he feared that his ex-wife was bad-mouthing him in front of their young, impressionable daughter. And he wasn't going to stand for it. But before he could get to the bottom of things, he had to make things right with Taylor. He couldn't risk losing her respect. "Baby girl, I messed up, but I'm going to make it up to you in a big way. I promise."

"Yeah, right, whatever," she drawled, wiping her eyes with the sleeve of her sweatshirt.

"Taylor, don't talk to me like that. I'm your father, and I love you—"

"Actions speak louder than words."

"I'm here, aren't I? There's nowhere else I'd rather be."

"Well, I don't want to be with you," Taylor shot back. "Just take me home."

"No. You're spending the weekend with me, and that's final."

"This is so unfair. You *never* listen to me. You only care about yourself."

"Honey, that isn't true," he said, hoping to get through to her. "You mean the world to me, and I'll do anything to make you happy."

Taylor snorted. "Yeah, right. If that was true, you wouldn't be forcing me to go to your boring bachelor pad. I hate that place."

There was a long, painful silence, and even the popular rap song playing on the car stereo couldn't cheer Max up. He felt dejected, like a failure as a father. And when Taylor put in her earbuds and closed her eyes, his heart sank to the bottom of his shoes. He needed help with his daughter and knew just whom to call.

Chapter 4

"I really outdid myself this time," Aubree Allen announced, with a proud smile. "I hate to toot my own horn, but I nailed Grandma Loretta's sugar cookie recipe!"

Skeptical, Jada dipped a spoon into the bowl of cookie batter, licked it and puckered her lips. "It's bitter." She grabbed her metal water bottle off the granite countertop inside her cousin's spacious kitchen and drank some ice-cold water. "I think you used too much lemon zest."

"Then I'll add a dash of wine to sweeten the recipe." Aubree opened the cupboard above the stove and rummaged around inside for several seconds. Raising an arm triumphantly in the air, she waved around the bottle. "A splash of zinfandel should do the trick."

Delilah Allen-Fayed, another cousin of Jada's, wrestled the bottle out of Aubree's hands and put it on the table. "We'll do no such thing," she hissed, an incredulous look on her face. "These Christmas cookies are for the Los Angeles Mission, not for dessert with the Book Club Divas, and I don't want us to get in trouble with Father Joseph."

"There's nothing wrong with a little wine. It's good for the heart *and* our sex drive."

"Then we're definitely not doing it," Jada said. "Kids are going to be eating these cookies, too, and I don't want them to get drunk."

"Gosh, Jada, you're such a killjoy!" Aubree complained, rolling her eyes to the ceiling. "Must you take the fun out of everything?"

"You're a fine one to talk," Jada shot back. "You're scared of heights and horror movies, and the last time you were on a plane Clinton was president!"

Erupting in laughter, Delilah gave Jada a high five. "Good one, cousin! *You* told her!"

Jada grabbed the wine bottle, marched into the pantry and put it on the top shelf. "Add some more milk to the batter," she advised Aubree, slamming the door shut. "And if that doesn't work put lots of icing on the cookies. No one will even notice they're sour."

Keeping an eye on what her wine-loving cousin was doing, Jada wiped the metal pan with butter. She grabbed a handful of dough, rolled it into a circle and dropped it onto the cookie sheet. That morning, after breakfast, she'd driven to Aubree's swank two-bedroom Malibu townhome to help bake holiday treats for the homeless shelter. While her cousins rolled the cinnamon buns, they discussed their plans for the Christmas holidays, their respective careers and relationships. Jada didn't have much to add to the conversation, but she enjoyed hearing about Aubree's dating woes and Delilah's storybook marriage. The stay-at-home mom had been married to an aircraft mechanic for a decade, and Delilah was so madly in love with her husband her face lit up every time she said his name.

Aubree, on the other hand, was single and actively looking for Mr. Right. The bold, brash graphic designer never left the house without makeup—not even to walk across the street to the community mailbox—and when it came to fashion, the thirty-year-old beauty never made a mistake. She looked chic in her printed silk headscarf, cashmere sweater and black, studded leggings, and Jada envied her cousin's effortless style.

Lightning lit up the dark, cloud-filled sky. Rain pelted the windows, and a strong breeze whipped tree branches in the air. From where she stood in the kitchen, Jada looked around at Aubree's living room. Adorned with pendant lamps, fuzzy pillows on velvet chairs and couches, and dozens of scented candles, the town house looked expensive and modern.

Working alongside, Aubree and Delilah reminded Jada of all the summers they'd spent together—watching MTV, pigging out on junk food, gossiping about their crushes and practicing the latest dance moves. In high school, Aubree had been voted most likely to succeed—and she had—and Delilah was the most loving wife and mother Jada knew.

"I went for a consultation at Malibu Fertility Center yesterday," Aubree announced.

Delilah snorted a laugh, dismissing the comment with a wave of her hand. "Sure you did, and on the weekends I moonlight as an exotic dancer at a gentlemen's club!"

"Why would I lie? One of my colleagues used the clinic last year and said it was the best decision she's ever made. Now she's six months pregnant and positively glowing."

"You want to be a mother?" Jada asked, flabbergasted by her cousin's words.

"Yes, of course. Why do you sound so surprised? You know me. We grew up together."

Eyes wide, Delilah wiped her hands on her apron. "*Exactly*—that's why we're stunned. No offense, coz, but you're the least maternal woman I know. You rarely babysit your nephews, and when you do you fuss and complain about every spill, runny nose and dirty diaper."

Aubree picked up the bowl now empty of cookie dough and chucked it in the sink. "That was then, and this is now."

"Girl, please," Delilah drawled. "That was a week ago, and if I didn't throw you out of my house you'd still be bitching and complaining about my amazing kids!"

"Talk to us. What's going on?" Jada asked, eager to get to the bottom of things. "Is this about Grayson's new girlfriend?"

An anguished expression pinched Aubree's face, but she shook her head. "No, of course not. Grayson's old news, and his fake-ass engagement has nothing to do with my decision."

"Okay," Delilah trilled. "But babies aren't puppies. When you change your mind, which you inevitably will, you can't take it back to the hospital. It doesn't work like that, Aubree."

Smirking, Aubree tilted her head to the right and fluttered her fake, extra-long eyelashes. "I know—don't worry. If I change my mind I'll just drop Aubree Junior off at your house!"

"You wish! You better give your kid to Jada, and

leave me be!" Delilah said, hitching a hand to her hips. "Gosh, you're worse than Ibrahim. He wants another baby and won't let up about it. I'm just not ready to get pregnant again, and I don't know if I'll ever be."

Aubree set the timer on the oven, then filled the mixing bowl with soapy water. "Really? But for as long as I can remember you've always wanted a big family, at least four or five kids."

"That was *before* I had two kids in three years."

Surprised by her cousin's harsh tone, Jada studied her closely. Her ponytail was crooked, dark circles lined her eyes, and there was a stain on her white scoop-neck top.

"Don't get me wrong," Delilah said with a sheepish smile. "I love my children, and wouldn't trade them for anything in the world, but motherhood isn't as fun as celebrity moms make it look. It's stressful, taxing and damn hard, if you ask me."

"I bet, and you didn't even get a push gift after giving birth to baby Hakeem." Aubree grabbed the coffeepot, filled three mugs and plopped down on one of the wooden stools at the breakfast bar. "It's not too late. Tell hubby you're not having another kid until he buys you diamond earrings and the new Hermès Birkin bag."

"As if! With me not working, it's hard to make ends meet, and I don't want Ibrahim to feel bad about our financial troubles. He's a good guy, and despite everything we've been through, he's my everything."

Delilah wrapped her hands around the ceramic mug. Her smile returned, shone brighter than the lights in the bronze chandelier hanging from the ceiling. Listening to her cousin gush about her husband made Jada think about Max and their nonexistent romantic relationship. An image of him popped into her mind, and her heart jolted inside her body. Jada knew she was out of Max's league, that he'd never settle down with a plain Jane from Inglewood who loved crossword puzzles, science fiction books and baking, but she couldn't stop herself from lusting after him. Having been Max's assistant for years, Jada knew him better than anyone, and it was obvious he had a penchant for actresses and models. Still, she couldn't stop fantasizing about him no matter how hard she tried.

"You guys, I need your help," Jada blurted out, desperate for her cousins' advice. "My feelings for Max have gotten stronger the last few months, and I don't know what to do to get his attention. I want him to notice me, but I'm fresh out of ideas."

Aubree and Delilah arched their eyebrows, and Jada wished she'd kept her thoughts to herself. Wished she hadn't confided in her cousins about her crush on her suave, debonair boss, because the skeptical expressions on their faces said they didn't believe in her.

"I'm not surprised. We've been telling you for *years* you need to update your look, but you won't listen to us," Delilah reminded her. "No makeover, no Max. It's just that simple."

"Those dowdy glasses? Get contacts. Your do-nothing hair? Extensions, girl, or get a chic, new cut! Those shapeless cardigans and ballet flats? Wear pencil skirts and stilettos!" Aubree advised. "Coz, you're hiding an amazing body under boring, frumpy clothes, and it's a damn shame, if you ask me."

Unconvinced, Jada vehemently disagreed with her cousins. She loved Aubree and Delilah, and valued their opinion, but she didn't want to change who she was to snag a guy—not even one she was crushing on.

"It's high time you got some." Delilah inclined her

head to the right and wiggled her eyebrows. "And if you revamp your look, men will be falling at your feet, including Max."

Jada had to admit she liked the sound of that. Just the thought of kissing Max made her skin tingle and her temperature rise. He was a force, the kind of man who could weaken a woman's resolve with just one smile, and his charming personality and go-getter attitude was a turn-on. And it didn't hurt that his hard, chiseled body was pure perfection.

"Jada, you need a makeover ASAP," Aubree stated in a curt, no-nonsense voice. "After the cookies are done we're going to Envy Beauty Salon to get your hair done, then shopping for some trendy, skintight clothes…"

Dread filled her body and pooled in the pit of her stomach. Shopping with her cousins was an all-day event—one that Jada didn't enjoy. They'd spend hours going in and out of high-end boutiques, trying on dresses and shoes they couldn't afford, despite her protests. Jada preferred going into Bloomingdale's, buying what she needed and going home. Not Aubree and Delilah. They treated shopping as if it was a professional sport, and Jada wanted no part of their Saturday afternoon outing to Rodeo Drive. "No way. I'm not going. I'm fine just the way I am—"

"Like hell you are," Aubree interrupted, her tone filled with attitude and sass. "You're going, even if we have to drag you out of here, kicking and screaming."

Delilah fervently nodded her head. "You need our help, and with the holidays right around the corner, it's the perfect time to unveil a sexy, new you, and we'll show you how."

Jada wanted to argue, but it was true; she didn't know anything about fashion trends. How could she? Helping to raise her siblings had left her no time to experiment with hairstyles, makeup or clothes. Hence her decision to keep her look simple—lip gloss, a cardigan, dress pants and ballet flats. Jada never deviated from the script, and even though Aubree and Delilah had been criticizing her wardrobe for years, she was scared to change her appearance.

Conflicted thoughts crowded her mind. What if she looked ridiculous? What if she hated her makeover, and Max did, too? She'd never be able to show her face at the office, and she didn't want to put her job in jeopardy. Jada loved being Max's administrative assistant, and wanted to work at Millennium Talent Agency for many more years to come. "I hate the idea of snaring Max through a dramatic, over-the-top holiday makeover," she confessed. "Shouldn't he fall for me because of who I am, not my hairstyle or clothes?"

Aubree scoffed. "In what world? Need I remind you that Max Moore is one of the hottest bachelors in LA? He's a sharp dresser with a handsome face and a rock-hard body."

"Is he frumpy?" Delilah asked, tossing an arm around Jada's shoulder. "No, so get with the times, girl. If you don't, someone will swoop in and steal him right from under your nose."

The thought of Max falling for another woman frightened Jada, and as much as she didn't want to admit it, her cousins were right. She had to act. Now. Before it was too late, and she lost Max forever. The problem was, Jada didn't know anything about making the first move, and wasn't confident enough to bare her soul to him. What if he rejected her? What if her confession ruined their relationship? Jada didn't know what to do, and struggled with following her heart. *Should I risk my career for love, or keep my mouth shut?*

"Jada, there's nothing wrong with having natural hair if you style it, but you never do." Delilah raised her mug to her mouth, blew in it, then took a sip. "I love you, girl, but you've been rocking the same, tired look for years, and you need to try something different."

"Or you'll remain a single, lonely virgin forever," Aubree warned.

Jade winced. She couldn't believe her loved ones could be so mean. She wanted to remind her know-it-all cousin that she was single, too, but before she could speak, the timer buzzed. Aubree hopped off her stool and rushed over to the stainless-steel stove.

Humming "Silent Night," Aubree slipped on silicone mitts, opened the oven and took out the cookie sheets one at a time. She put the racks on the stove, then helped herself to a cookie. "These are *so* good," she gushed, slowly licking her lips.

Jada's cell phone rang, and she picked it up from the counter. Frowning, she stared at the number on the screen. She didn't understand why Max was calling on her day off. Unless… Fear gripped her heart. Had his father passed away? Did he need her support?

Clearing her throat, she put her cell to her ear and spoke in a confident tone of voice, even though her mouth was bone-dry. "Hey, Max, how are you? Everything okay?"

"No. Taylor got mad at me yesterday, and twenty-four hours later she's still giving me the silent treatment," he explained in a somber tone of voice. "Needless to say, it sucks."

Relief flowed through Jada's body, and a sigh fell from her lips.

"I apologized, and even ordered pizza for dinner, but she's still in a miserable funk."

"I'm sorry to hear that," she said, unsure of what else to say. "That's rough."

"Tell me about it. I feel like a visitor in my own home, and the silence is killing me."

"Is there anything I can do to help?"

"I'm glad you asked. I'm taking Taylor to FunZone Galaxy this afternoon, and I'd love if you could join us. My daughter enjoys your company, and so do I. Please say you'll come."

His words warmed her heart, and a smile curled her lips. "I... I—I'd love to," Jada stammered. Thrilled Max had asked her out, she wanted to dance around her cousin's apartment. Sure, it wasn't an official date, but he'd never included her in a family outing before, and his invitation made Jada feel special.

"Great! Thanks, Jada. I knew I could count on you. You're a lifesaver..."

And you're the dreamiest man I've ever met.

"We'll pick you up from your condo at two o'clock. How does that sound?"

"I'll be waiting," Jada said, surging to her feet. "See you then!"

Ending the call, she grabbed her purse off the couch, waved goodbye to her cousins and made a beeline for the door. They followed her through the living room, asking a million questions about her mysterious phone call, but Jada was so hyped about seeing Max on her day off, nothing could spoil her good mood. "I'll give you guys a ring later."

"Where do you think you're going?" Aubree asked, thwarting Jada's escape by positioning herself in front of the door. "You can't bail on us. We're supposed to drop the cookies off at the homeless shelter, then get our hair and nails done."

"I know, but I have to go. Max needs me. It's important."

Delilah sucked her teeth. "Oh, so Max calls and you go running?"

Yeah, pretty much. He's my boss, and I'll do anything for him!

"I'll make it up to you guys, I promise," Jada vowed. "Give my love to Father Joseph, take tons of pictures with the kids we mentor at Tween Connection and enjoy your day of beauty!"

Aubree opened the closet, grabbed an umbrella off the top shelf and handed it to Jada. "Here, use this. We don't want you to look a mess when you meet up with your fine-ass boss."

Jada giggled. "Thanks, girl. I owe you one."

"Call us later." Aubree unlocked the door. "We want to know how your date went."

"It's not a date," Jada said, pulling up the collar on her denim jacket. "His daughter is coming with us to the arcade."

"Then be creative," Delilah advised, her eyes bright with mischief. "Go home with them, and help him put his daughter to bed. After she falls asleep, lure Max into the master bedroom, lock the door and handcuff him to the headboard..."

"Now I know why Ibrahim popped the question after dating you for only three months," Jada joked, swatting her cousin playfully on the shoulder. "You're a freak!"

Taking a deep breath, Jada threw open the screen door. She sprinted down the walkway, careful to avoid the mud puddles dotting the sidewalk. Running full speed toward her black Nissan parked across the street,

Jada could feel water in her shoes. The strong wind ripped the umbrella from her hands, and rain pelted her cold, quivering body.

Reaching the car, Jada got in and collapsed against the seat. She stared at her reflection in the rearview mirror and groaned. Water was dripping down her face, her hair was sticking to her cheeks and neck, and her sweatshirt clung to her skin.

Wanting to freshen up before Max and Taylor arrived, Jada put on her seat belt, started the car and drove slowly through the apartment complex. Like her hair, her shoes were soaking wet, but hanging out with Max was worth every inconvenience. And if Jada had her way, this would be the first of many Saturday afternoon dates with her boss and his adorable daughter.

Considering what her cousins said, Jada decided it was time to make her move. To tell Max the truth. To bare her soul to him. She smacked the gas pedal with her foot and sped through the intersection, anxious to see the man she loved. Jada only hoped that when she told Max how she felt about him he wouldn't reject her. Or worse, laugh in her face.

Chapter 5

The buzzer on top of the arcade game Half Court Hoops sounded and Max sprang to action. Grabbing one of the small orange basketballs in the cage, he arched his arms and shot at the miniature net. It fell in, and his confidence soared. Determined to win, Max focused on making every bucket, even though his limbs were still sore from playing dodgeball with Taylor and Jada earlier.

FunZone Galaxy was a family-friendly establishment, with a bowling alley, gymnasium, go-kart racing, a snack shop and a small restaurant. It was a paradise on earth for entertainment lovers, and the striking black-and-gold decor gave the space a unique look. They'd been at FunZone for hours, and Max was so hungry his stomach was moaning and groaning. The arcade smelled of popcorn and cotton candy, and his mouth watered at the delicious aromas in the air. Filled with teenagers, birthday party guests and children racing from one game to the next, the place was noisy and crowded, but Max was having a great time with his daughter and wasn't ready to leave.

Moving at lightning-quick speed, he made one basket after another. He watched Jada on the sly, noticed her careful, precise movements. She wasn't wearing makeup, her eyeglasses were perched on the tip of her nose, and her thick black hair was pulled back in its trademark bun. Her polka-dot sweater and capri pants gave her a serious, mature appearance, but she had a fierce expression on her pretty, heart-shaped face. "Jada, give up while you still have a chance, because there's no way in hell I'm letting you beat me…"

Max tried to rattle Jada by cracking jokes, but she never took her eyes off the basketball net, focused in on it like a laser beam. Playing against his assistant was fun, and listening to Taylor's colorful commentary made Max laugh out loud. His daughter was a character, hands down the funniest kid he knew, and he loved her sense of humor.

Down five points, Max hurried to catch up. Jada had easily won the first round, and he had to redeem himself. He couldn't let his perky, petite assistant beat him twice. If she did, Taylor would tease him mercilessly for the rest of the weekend, and Max couldn't think of anything worse than his tween daughter poking fun at him. "Jada, you're toast," he shouted over the loud pop song playing on the stereo system. "You're going down."

"You wish!" she shot back. "I beat you once, and I'll do it again. Just watch."

Taylor cupped her hands around her mouth. "You can do it, Ms. Jada! I believe in you!"

Max glanced over his shoulder, caught his daughter's eye and faked a scowl. It was hard not to crack up when

Taylor was jumping around the arcade like a kangaroo, but he wore a straight face. "Traitor. Keep it up, and I'm not buying you dinner."

"Sweetie, don't worry," Jada said with a wink and a smile. "I got you. Pizza's on me."

"Thanks, Ms. Jada. You're the best! Not like my dad. He's *so* sensitive."

The buzzer sounded, the score flashed on the screen and Max plucked the collar of his navy button-down shirt. "I *told* you guys I'd win," he said.

Jada shrugged a shoulder. "Lucky shot. It could happen to anyone."

"You're just mad because I won. Better luck next time, Brown Eyes!"

Taylor linked arms with Max and Jada, and gestured with her head to the other side of the arcade. "Let's play *Dance Dance Revolution* and *Guitar Hero*. They're my favorite games."

"*After* we eat." Max walked into the restaurant, dropped down at one of the vinyl booths and grabbed a menu. "You've been dragging us around this place all afternoon, and if I don't eat something soon, I'm going to get hangry, and it'll be all your fault."

Taylor didn't laugh at his joke. "Fine, Dad, you can eat, but we're going to dance."

"I'm going to take a break, too," Jada said. "I'm starving."

"But I want to play more games," Taylor argued.

"Fine, don't eat," Max said, perusing the menu. "Sit down and keep us company."

Breathless, Jada collapsed in the seat. "We'll take a short break, and as soon as I'm finished eating I'm all yours. We can play *DDR* a million times if you want."

Wearing a long face, Taylor sat down beside Jada and crossed her arms.

Max swallowed the words on the tip of his tongue. His daughter was pouting, acting like a spoiled brat because she didn't get her way, but he ignored her behavior. Pretended not to notice her pursed lips and rigid posture. They'd had a great afternoon, and he didn't want anything to ruin their outing. He rarely hung out with Jada socially, and he enjoyed learning more about her. As usual, she'd come to his rescue, and for the first time since Max learned of his father's illness, he could breathe. He didn't feel as if a boulder was sitting on his chest, slowly suffocating him.

Max studied Jada from behind his menu. All afternoon, she'd been sympathetic and supportive, there for him when he'd needed it most. While watching Taylor play *Donkey Kong*—a game he'd played hundreds of times with his mom in their home media room when he was a kid—he'd found himself thinking about Constance. As if reading his thoughts, Jada had leaned in close and patted his forearm. "You must miss your mom," she'd said, in a soft, quiet tone of voice. "Cherish your memories, and honor her legacy by being the man and father she'd want you to be." Comforted by her words, he'd given her a one-arm hug. Max thanked his lucky stars that she was his ace assistant. Over the years, she'd changed from a shy, insecure woman to a confident beauty, and he valued her opinion above everyone else's at the agency. She thought for herself instead of relying on other people's opinions, and her candor was refreshing. Max liked having her around and looked forward to seeing her every morning. Jada made his life easier, calmed him down when he was upset, and best of all, she had a terrific relationship with his daughter.

"I don't know what to order," Jada said, studying the laminated menu with a furrowed brow. "Taylor, what do you recommend?"

Dropping her hands in her lap, the tween moved closer to Jada in the booth, chattering excitedly about her favorite drinks and appetizers from the snack bar.

Anxious to eat, Max signaled to the waiter wiping tables nearby. He ordered appetizers, pitchers of soda, three Caesar salads, and the pizzas Taylor and Jada wanted.

Using his iPhone discreetly under the table, Max checked his email. He tried not to work when Taylor was around, but he had dozens of messages, and he didn't want his celebrity clients to think he was ignoring them. His job was never-ending and consumed every area of his life. When he wasn't negotiating deals, fielding offers or meeting with clients for lunch and dinner, he was answering phone calls and text messages by the hundreds.

"I'm so pumped about Christmas it's all I can think about," Taylor confessed, giggling.

Max kept his head down, listened with half an ear as his daughter shared about upcoming events at her school and her three-page Christmas list. Settling back comfortably into his seat, he crossed his legs at the ankles and read a movie script on his cell phone.

His mind wandered, and the words blurred on the screen. It was hard to concentrate on work when all he could think about was his dad. That morning, he'd talked to his stepsister, Bianca, and found himself tearing up as they reminisced about their favorite childhood memories. They'd always been close, and Max wished

Bianca was around to help him with Reginald. An Ivy League graduate, Bianca was a successful software developer in New Hampshire, and Max was proud of everything she'd accomplished. His stepsister was coming to town for the holidays, and Max couldn't wait to see the look on Reginald's face when Bianca arrived at the Prescott George charity gala on Christmas Eve.

A waitress with tanned skin and wavy hair arrived with the drinks and appetizers, but the script was so intriguing Max didn't want to stop to eat. The waitress batted her eyelashes, but he pretended not to notice her coy smile. He was with his daughter, and he didn't want to encourage the waitress's advances. Though he enjoyed flirting with the opposite sex, it wasn't the time or the place. Playing the field would never get old, and although he envied his brothers for finding smart, captivating women with model good looks, Max had no desire to settle down. Romantic relationships were damn hard, and he didn't have the temperament for them. Couldn't see himself ever getting married again. Once was more than enough.

Thankful that Jada was keeping Taylor occupied, he read the second page of the script and made several comments in the margin. Blown away by how interesting the characters were, he made a mental note to call the up-and-coming screenwriter after Taylor went to bed. Would do everything in his power to sign her to his agency. He'd fulfilled, many times over, his hopes and dreams for his company, but it was never enough. A self-proclaimed workaholic, Max was always looking for the next big thing, the next blockbuster movie or breakout star, and was never satisfied with his success. Always wanted more. Millennium Talent Agency was one of the fastest-growing agencies in LA, but he wanted to increase company revenue next year and prove to his critics that it was a varied and versatile agency. To do that, he'd have to sign talent in all areas of entertainment, including publishing, theater, sports and advertising. It was going to be tough, but Max was up for the challenge. More than anything, he wanted to cement his place in Hollywood as a powerhouse who made things happen. And he would, even if it meant outwitting the competition.

"How are things going at school?" Jada asked. "Still loving the fifth grade?"

"Oh, yes," Taylor gushed, in a high-pitched voice. "I *love* school. My crush sits next to me now, and we talk and laugh all the time. To be honest, he's the best thing about school…"

Max glanced up from his cell phone. In his haste to speak, he tripped over his tongue, and his daughter stared at him as if he'd lost his mind.

"Max, are you okay?" Jada wore a concerned expression on her face. "You look upset."

"Damn right, I'm upset." Pocketing his cell phone, he spoke in a stern tone of voice. "Taylor, you're too young to have a crush. You're only ten years old. Furthermore, your mom and I send you to school to get an education, not drool over boys."

"TaVonte is wonderful." Stars twinkled in her eyes, and a lopsided smile curled her lips. "He's the smartest kid in my class, and the nicest, too—"

"TaVonte?" Max repeated, cutting her off. "What kind of name is that?"

Taylor picked up a mozzarella stick and took a bite. "Dad, you don't know him, so stop throwing shade. I think it's a cute name. Just like TaVonte."

"I think I'm going to be sick," he grumbled, feeling

an ache in his stomach. "I *knew* we should have enrolled you in the Malibu Girls Academy, but your mom wouldn't listen to me."

"I'm glad she didn't. If I was at a private school, I wouldn't have met TaVonte…"

Taylor sighed in relief, infuriating him, and it took everything in Max not to curse.

The waitress returned with the salads and pizza but he'd lost his appetite. Jada encouraged him to try her honey barbecue wings, but eating was the last thing on his mind. All he could think about was getting through to his daughter. And he would, because he didn't want history to repeat itself. Shay had gotten pregnant on prom night, at just eighteen years old, and even though Max didn't regret having Taylor, he didn't want her to make the same mistake. He wanted her to go to university, travel the world and work in her desired field, without anything ever holding her back.

"Everyone at school calls us T and T, even our homeroom teacher. Adorable, right?"

"No," Max snapped, leaning forward in his seat. "You need to focus on your studies, not boys. You're only ten, for goodness' sake! A baby!"

"Dad, I'm ten and a half. Get it right," she scolded, reaching for her glass.

An Arab girl wearing a pink hijab, a cropped hoodie and high-waist jeans stopped in front of their table. "Hi, Taylor! Want to play flag tag in the gym with me and my cousins?"

"Dad, I'm finished eating. Can I go?" Taylor wiped her hands with a napkin. "Please?"

Max hesitated. He didn't want his daughter hanging out with teenagers, or making friends with the high school boys playing basketball in the gym. "Sure, but stay with your friend. No wandering off," he said, glancing at his Rolex wristwatch. "Be back at six o'clock."

Taylor cocked her head. "That's not enough time for us to hang out."

Annoyed, Max stared intently at his daughter. *Is this kid for real?*

"You guys can leave when you're ready. I'll just ask Nawal's parents to drop me home later." Standing, she slung her beanbag purse over her shoulder. "I'm sure Mr. and Mrs. Almasi won't mind. Nawal and I are practically besties."

"No, you'll be back in an hour, or you can stay here."

Taylor started to argue, but Max silenced her with a look, and she closed her open mouth.

"Fine, I'll be back at six."

Whispering to each other, the tweens left.

"Do you see what I'm talking about?" Max asked, unable to conceal his frustration, his anger finally bubbling to the surface. "Taylor used to be a sweet girl who listened to her parents, but now she's argumentative, disrespectful and obsessed with boys."

"Max, calm down. You're shouting, and people are staring at us—"

"Of course I'm shouting! My ten-year-old daughter is out of control. 'Everyone at school calls us T and T,'" he mimicked, adopting a high-pitched female voice. "What kind of nonsense is that? I have half a mind to call the school and complain."

Jada set aside her plate, took a sip of her soda, then clasped her hands in front of her. "Max, I know your relationship with your daughter is none of my business, and it doesn't matter what I think, but can I be honest with you?"

"Please. That's why I invited you here. I need your help to get through to Taylor."

"But Taylor isn't the problem," Jada said, looking him in the eye. "You are."

Chapter 6

"Come again?" Max asked, pointing a finger at his chest. "You think *I'm* the problem? How do you figure? I'm not the one with the bad attitude."

Jada swallowed hard. Pretended not to notice the peeved expression on Max's face. He was glaring at her as if they were enemies. Had she said too much? Overstepped her bounds? They'd spent the afternoon playing games and goofing around in the gym, and the last thing Jada wanted to do was ruin his good mood.

Jada could feel her heart beating in double time, and her pulse throbbing in her ears, but she said, "Let me explain."

"Please do because I'm dying to know what I'm doing wrong."

"Max, it's obvious you love your daughter more than anything, but you treat her like she's five years old, and she's not a little girl anymore. She's a tween who's changing in many different ways, and it's perfectly normal."

He was quick to say, "I don't have a problem with Taylor growing up. I have a problem with her chasing boys instead of doing her schoolwork."

"You overreacted about Taylor having a crush, and it hurt her feelings."

"What was I supposed to do? Tell her to invite the kid over for dinner?"

"That's a start. Taylor's going to be a teenager before you know it, and it would be wise to get to know the kids she hangs out with."

Inclining his head, Max wore a thoughtful expression on his face.

"When Taylor confides in you and you shut her down, you're damaging your relationship," Jada pointed out, feeling compelled to speak her mind. All afternoon, she'd fantasized about them being her family—her gorgeous husband, Max, and her precocious stepdaughter, Taylor—and wanted to help out any way she could. The truth was, Jada wanted her own family, wanted it all with Max. She'd been secretly in love with him for a long time, and spending quality time with her humorous, fun-loving boss made her desire him even more. He wasn't perfect, but he was perfect for her, and no one else could ever take his place in her heart.

"What do you suggest I do?"

"Be transparent," she advised. "The next time Taylor opens up to you about a problem she's having with a friend, or about someone she has a crush on, just listen. Don't react. If you lose your temper every time she confides in you, you'll never have a healthy relationship."

Max took a breadstick out of the plastic basket and broke it in half. "Taylor shouldn't be obsessing over boys. She should be riding her bike and playing with dolls…"

Memories flooded Jada's mind. As a child, she'd always wished she could do fun things with her dad, like going bowling or to the movies, but he'd never had the time or money to take her. "You're getting worked up over nothing. It's a harmless crush, and nothing more."

"That's easy for you to say. You don't have kids."

"Oh, so because I don't have kids I can't have an opinion about a healthy parent-child relationship?" Jada asked, irked by his flippant remark.

Max shrugged a shoulder. "Yeah, pretty much."

"That's ridiculous. I've always had a great relationship with my dad—"

"I believe you, but you're a pretty, young woman who knows nothing about kids."

His words gave her a rush. *You think I'm pretty?*

"Normally, you're bang on about Taylor, but this time you're dead wrong."

Jada swiped a napkin off the table, scrunched it into a ball and tossed it at Max.

Chuckling, he swatted it to the floor. "What? Don't get mad. I'm just keeping it real."

"No," she argued, fighting the urge to laugh. "You're terrible, that's what you are."

Max picked up a slice of pizza, took a bite and chewed slowly, as if he was savoring the taste. "I know you mean well, and I appreciate your advice, but Taylor isn't going to date until she's thirty, and that's final," he said, with an arch grin.

As they ate, Max opened up to Jada about his family meeting the day before at his father's estate. He held nothing back, confided in her about his father's declining health, his fears of losing Reginald during the holidays, and his improved relationship with his brothers.

Jada propped her chin in her hand. It was hard not to admire his handsome face and his broad shoulders. Her hands were itching to squeeze them, but Jada exercised self-control. Forgetting everyone else in the room, she blocked out the boisterous chatter, laughter and music around her and concentrated on what he was saying. Jada could listen to Max talk all night. Couldn't take her eyes off him. Captivated by the sound of his voice, Jada imagined herself leaning across the table and kissing him. She could see it now—their lips mating, their tongues teasing and exploring, their hands caressing each other—and trembled at the thought. Her nipples hardened under her blouse, yearned for his touch, and it took everything in Jada not to pounce on him. She'd never felt such intense feelings for a man and hoped she didn't do anything to embarrass herself.

"Did you hear back from the event planner? Can she plan the office Christmas party, or do we have to hire someone else?"

Jada was so busy fantasizing about Max she didn't hear what he'd said, and felt like an idiot when he waved his hands in front of her face and repeated the question. Meeting his gaze to assure him she hadn't taken leave of her senses, Jada nodded in response. "Everything's been taken care of," she said brightly, remembering the conversation she'd had with the celebrity event planner yesterday afternoon. "We're good to go."

"Awesome. I invited my brothers and their fiancées and several of my business associates to the party as well, so make sure you touch base with the caterer on Monday to confirm the number of guests. I'd hate for us to run out of food or drinks at the office party."

On the outside, Jada was smiling, but on the inside dread pooled inside her stomach. Jada had no interest in attending the office Christmas party, and considered faking an injury. Her colleagues were bringing their significant others to the event, and she'd be the only one without a date. Thankfully, she'd had strep throat last year and couldn't attend the party, but she'd heard from the staff how Max's pop-star girlfriend had stolen the show in her cut-out dress and seductive dance moves. Jada would rather eat broken glass than watch Max make out with his date, and made up her mind to stay home next Friday.

"I look forward to meeting the special man in your life." Max took another slice of pizza, folded it in half and took a bite. "Tell me more about your boyfriend."

Jada felt her mouth drop open and quickly slammed it shut. She wasn't used to having his undivided attention, couldn't recall him ever asking her about her love life in the two years she'd been his assistant. He was always on his cell, texting, talking and Tweeting, and her colleagues often joked about him being obsessed with his iPhone. Jada relished their newfound friendship. They were closer than they'd ever been, and even though she was nervous about baring her soul to Max, it was time to come clean. "I'm not seeing anyone right now," she blurted out. "I'd rather read than peruse cheesy dating apps."

"That's a shame. A beautiful woman like you should be going out on the weekends, exploring the incredible LA nightlife, not sitting at home twiddling her thumbs."

I agree! But the only *man I want to spend my evenings with is you!* For several seconds, Jada mentally rehearsed what she wanted to say. Choosing her words carefully, she met his gaze and forced the truth out of her mouth. "I've been interested in someone for a long time, but up until now I was too afraid to say anything—"

Max peered over her shoulder, and Jada lost her train of thought. She was so distracted by his wandering eye that her confidence deserted her, and she broke off speaking. Max straightened in his chair, and Jada knew there was an attractive woman standing behind her. Had to be. Why else would he be straining his neck?

Frustrated that he wasn't listening to her, Jada glanced over her shoulder to see who the object of his attention was and widened her eyes. Max wasn't lusting after a female; he was watching a tender, heartwarming scene. A silver-haired man was holding a toddler in his arms, laughing uncontrollably. Singing a nursery rhyme at the top of her lungs, the blue-eyed girl smacked his cheeks with her chubby hands, then pinched his crooked nose.

Turning back around, Jada noticed the pensive expression on Max's face and instinctively reached for his hand. A soft sigh escaped her lips. *This is heaven on earth!* Jada liked feeling his skin against hers, enjoyed stroking his soft, smooth flesh with her fingertips. It was obvious Max was thinking about when Taylor was a toddler, and it saddened her that he was in pain. Jada didn't know what to say to make him feel better and searched her heart for the right words. Her confession would have to wait. Max wasn't in the right frame of mind to have an open and honest conversation about their relationship, and Jada wanted them to talk when he was in a good mood, not when he was stressed out.

Her gaze dropped from his eyes to his mouth, and a shiver shot down her spine. The desire to kiss him was so overwhelming, Jada couldn't think of anything else. She'd wanted him from the day she'd first laid eyes on him, and didn't know how much longer she could resist the needs of her flesh.

Get a hold of yourself, woman! chided her inner voice, in a stern, no-nonsense tone. *Max needs to be comforted right now, not seduced, so back off!*

The waitress returned to clear the dishes and wipe down the dirty table.

"Thanks," Max said. "Everything was great tonight, especially the service."

"It was my pleasure," the redhead cooed, sticking out her chest. "Anything else?"

"No, thanks. Just the bill."

The waitress didn't move and continued to stare at Max with lust in her eyes. Jada didn't blame her for flirting with him. It happened all the time. His clean-cut good looks and boyish smile drove women wild, and Max couldn't go anywhere without attracting female attention. It didn't help that he was Mr. Personality, and when his business associates teased him for being a ladies' man he'd wink and chuckle, as if every salacious rumor about him was true.

Max's cell phone buzzed, and he scooped it up off the table. A slow smile crept across his lips, and Jada suspected he was reading a text message from one of his girlfriends.

"Derek and Alexis are the most," he joked with an amused expression on his face. "Alexis is only in her first trimester, but they've already finished decorating the Disney-themed nursery at my brother's Malibu estate."

Max held up his iPhone, and Jada stared at the image on the screen. The bright, spacious room had stuffed animals, jumbo alphabet letters, colored blocks and wooden shelves lined with toys, picture books and family photographs. "Talk about efficient," Jada said in an awe-filled voice. "If I ever have a baby, I want Derek and Alexis to decorate the nursery!"

The grin slid off his mouth, and he raised an eyebrow. "I hope you're not thinking of settling down and having kids anytime soon. Are you?"

Something told her not to speak, so she didn't respond to the question.

"I hope not, because I need you at Millennium Talent Agency. You do a kick-ass job at the office, and I couldn't survive a day without you, let alone three months."

"I absolutely want to be a wife and mother, and the sooner, the better, but don't worry, Max. I'll give you plenty of notice before I run off to the suburbs and set up house."

"Can I give you some advice?"

Before Jada could respond, Max gave her his take on relationships. And what he said shattered her hope of them ever being a couple. Heartbroken, her head bent, she stared down at her hands. Jada was so disappointed she couldn't look at Max. She feared if she did she'd burst into tears. Based on comments she'd overheard him make in the past, Jada knew his views about love and relationships were tainted by his divorce, but she didn't realize he was anti-commitment, anti-marriage and dead set against having more children. *I've been fooling myself all this time*, Jada thought, wanting to flee the restaurant. *How could I have been so stupid? Max doesn't want me, and he never will.*

"I'm not trying to burst your bubble, Jada, but relationships are a waste of time."

Staring off into space, he seemed to be in another world, and his anger was evident by his tone.

"Happily-ever-after is a myth, a fallacy used to sell movies, books and engagement rings, and if you don't abandon the ridiculous notion of finding your soul mate and riding off into the sunset, you'll wind up being miserable and disappointed."

Too late for that. I already am, she thought sourly, a bitter taste filling her mouth. Jada felt low, as if someone had ripped her heart out of her chest and stomped all over it, but she found the courage to ask the question in her mind. "Do you plan to spend the rest of your life alone?"

"Maybe one day, when I'm old and gray, I'll find love again. Never say never, right?" His laugh was hollow. "Settling down is the last thing on my mind right now. I like my life just the way it is, and I have my hands full with Taylor, work, my family and Prescott George."

"Humor me," she said, curious to know more about the man behind the dashing, larger-than-life persona. "What kind of woman could take you off the market permanently?"

Max didn't speak for a long moment, then surprised her by answering the question.

"Someone humble, loyal and sincere," he began. "I want to be with a woman who enjoys the simple things in life, like breakfast in bed, long scenic drives, picnics in the park and afternoons binge-watching classic TV shows."

Max, I love all those things, and I love— Jada stopped herself from finishing the thought. He didn't want her, never would. Their mutual attraction had been nothing more than a figment of her imagination, and it was time to quit pining over him. Now that it was clear they'd never be a couple, or have the relationship Jada had always dreamed of, she had to move on. It was going to be hard, especially after the heartfelt conversation they'd had during dinner, but Jada wasn't going to waste another second of her life on a man who obviously didn't want her.

"Look what I won at Treasure Quest!" Taylor sidled up to the table with a bright smile, clutching a brown teddy bear. "I named him TaVonte Jr. Isn't he cute?"

Jada saw the color drain from Max's face and hoped he didn't lose his temper again. "Did you have fun with your friends in the gym?" she asked, cleaning her sticky hands with a napkin.

"Yeah, Nawal and I creamed her cousins at dodgeball. One of the guys nicknamed me *La Bestia*, which means 'The Beast' in Spanish, because of my strong right arm."

Max stood and gave Taylor a one-arm hug. "That's my girl! Show no mercy!"

"Dad, you'd be so proud of me. I knocked out most of the players by myself."

"Way to go, Taylor. Your opponent's right. You *are* a beast."

Max retrieved his leather wallet from his back pocket, took out three twenty-dollar bills and put them on the plastic bill tray. "Are we ready to go?"

"Dad, can we stop at Creams and Dreams on the way home?" Closing her eyes, Taylor licked her lips and rubbed her stomach. "I'm craving cookies-and-cream ice cream."

The waitress returned, scooped up the bill and thanked Max for his generous tip. Heading for the exit, Max took his car keys out of his pocket. The rain had stopped, but the cold, blustery wind was still battering trees along Lincoln Boulevard.

"Jada, is it okay with you if we make a quick detour

for dessert?" Max asked, opening the passenger-side door. "*La Bestia* wants a sweet treat, and if I say no she'll give me a beatdown."

Taylor giggled, and the sound of her girlish laughter warmed Jada's heart. She glanced at Max and could tell by the light in his eyes that he felt the same way. Father and daughter were both in a playful mood, but Jada didn't feel like joking around, was ready to call it a night. She wanted to return to her condo, climb into bed and sleep until she forgot what Max had said about relationships.

As she replayed their conversation in her mind, her disappointment was so profound she couldn't look at Max. She wondered if she'd ever get over him. She'd spent months obsessing over a man who'd never give her the time of day, but enough was enough. No more fantasizing about him, doodling his name inside her journal or staring at pictures of him online.

A troubling thought came to mind, one Jada didn't have an answer to. *How am I supposed to overcome my feelings for Max when all I can think about is kissing him?* Tears pricked the backs of her eyes. She hadn't been this upset since Braydon dumped her, but she had to maintain her composure. Didn't want Max to know anything was wrong. Jada loved her job and it didn't matter how much she was hurting inside; she'd never do anything to embarrass him or jeopardize her position at Millennium Talent Agency.

"Please, Ms. Jada?" Taylor begged, clasping her hands together. "I promise to be good."

"Sweetie, don't be silly. You're *always* good. I'm just tired, that's all."

"Then we should definitely go to Creams and Dreams,"

Taylor said in a matter-of-fact tone of voice, wiggling her eyebrows. "Ice cream makes everything better!"

To make Taylor happy she agreed to join them at the ice-cream parlor, but as Jada put on her seat belt, she decided this would be her last outing with the Moore family. There'd be no more dates at the arcade or for ice cream, and even though Jada wanted to spend more time with the lovable father-daughter duo, her heart couldn't take it. It was going to hurt like hell, but she'd rather be alone than chase a man who didn't want her.

Chapter 7

Speed-walking along Hollywood Boulevard on Wednesday afternoon with Max's dry cleaning in one hand and her cell phone in the other, Jada mentally reviewed everything she had to do when she returned to the office. She had to order stationery and other supplies, organize the slide show for the conference Max was speaking at in San Francisco tomorrow, and touch base with the party planner about some last-minute details for the office Christmas party on Friday.

As she sweated profusely in her cashmere sweater and pleated skirt, perspiration drenched her skin, causing her eyeglasses to slide down her nose. Pushing them back in place, she narrowly avoided colliding with the teenagers dancing in front of the Palace Theater Building and hurried up the block. It had been a long, stressful week, and all Jada wanted to do was go home, kick off her shoes and stretch out on the couch to watch her favorite reality show, *Extreme Dating*. She had no plans, no dates, and even though Aubree claimed to have the "perfect" guy for her, Jada didn't want to meet her cousin's friend at a local bar. She couldn't think of anything more depressing than going on a blind date, and no matter how much Aubree badgered her about it, she wasn't having drinks with the Sacramento-based construction worker. Not because he had a blue-collar job, but because her heart belonged to Max, and even though she'd vowed to quit pining over him, he still dominated her thoughts.

Jada stopped at the intersection and waited impatiently for the traffic light to change. The air smelled of flowers and pine, and everywhere Jada looked, there were Christmas-themed signs and decorations. Lampposts were swathed in garland, trees were decorated with jumbo ornaments, and red satin ribbons hung in store windows. Christmas was three weeks away, but Jada could hear the distant sound of bells and saw a man of Asian descent dressed in a velvet Santa Claus costume standing on the street corner begging for change as he sang an off-key rendition of "We Wish You a Merry Christmas."

Her thoughts wandered, filled with images of her tall, dark and sexy boss. For the past five days, she'd replayed her conversation with Max at the arcade in her mind a million times, but it was time to let it go. Needed to find someone who shared her hopes and dreams. A man who'd be proud to claim her as his girl and show her off to his family and friends. Jada wanted it all—a loving marriage, a large family, a house with a white picket fence in the suburbs—and she refused to settle for anything else. And that was why she had to forget about Max.

Her cell phone buzzed, the screen lit up, and a smile filled her lips as she read her cousin's newest text message. Their hour-long conversation that morning had lifted Jada's spirits. During her commute to the office, she'd called Delilah, and listening to her cousin gush about her husband had made Jada envious. Made her wish she had a special man who brought her breakfast in bed, too. Delilah had advised her to forget about Max and have a Christmas fling, and Jada had to admit it sounded like a good idea. She had to get him out of her system. She'd never had a one-night stand, but Jada had to do something drastic to get over Max. *Yes*, she decided, fervently nodding her head. *A Christmas fling is* just *what the doctor ordered.*

A shiny black SUV with tinted windows and chrome wheels sped up to the curb. Afraid it would splash in the puddles and ruin her outfit, Jada jumped back and put the garment bag behind her. Doing personal errands for Max during her lunch break wasn't part of her official duties, but he was stuck in meetings all afternoon, and Jada didn't mind helping out. Without looking up from his iPhone, he'd handed her his platinum credit card, asked her to pick up his dry cleaning and requested Vietnamese food for lunch. His fingers had brushed against hers, arousing her flesh with just one touch. Electricity had shot through her veins, leaving her dizzy and weak. And when Max flashed a smile of thanks, she had to fight the urge to climb onto his lap and rip his suit from his body. Max was so fine he made *People* magazine's Sexiest Man Alive look homely, and if Jada didn't love her job—and her salary—she'd kiss him until she was breathless.

"Are you following me? First, I run into you at the dry cleaners, and now you're standing across the street from my favorite coffee shop, staring at me with lust in your eyes."

Am not! The deep, boisterous voice belonged to Shazir Toussiant, and as the talent agent climbed out of the SUV, her heart thumped inside her chest. She'd met Shazir last year at the Prescott George Christmas Eve charity fund-raiser, and since his office was only blocks away from Millennium Talent Agency, she bumped into him on a regular basis.

"Jada, you don't have to follow me around town," Shazir said smoothly. "If you want my number all you have to do is ask for it."

"I don't have time to follow you around. I'm a very busy woman," she quipped, trying not to notice how attractive he looked in his navy suit. "I have several more errands to run, so if you'll excuse me, I have to go."

Shazir slid in front of Jada, blocking her path, his boyish smile on full blast. "Not so fast, pretty lady. I have a weakness for women in cardigans, so you're not going anywhere until you agree to have dinner with me."

Amused, Jada stared at the pretty-boy bachelor with growing interest. With his soulful brown eyes, high cheekbones and dimpled chin, Shazir could easily have a career as a Disney prince. Admiring his striking facial features, Jada wondered if everything the talent scouts at Millennium had said was true. Did Shazir have a bad reputation? Did he hook up with his female employees? Did he play mind games with the opposite sex?

Jada broke free of her thoughts, told herself it didn't matter. She wasn't inviting Shazir back to her place for a passionate afternoon of lovemaking. They were just flirting, and Jada enjoyed their fun, playful banter. She sensed his interest in her and was flattered by his attention. Jada couldn't remember the last time she'd been on a date, and liked the idea of hanging out with the successful talent agent. Why not? She had nothing else to do on the weekend and hoped Shazir would give her some insight about Max. After all, they were members of the same exclusive club and had known each other for more than a decade. "Shouldn't you be off somewhere searching for the next big child star?"

"It can wait. Gotta get your digits first."

Jada smirked. She couldn't resist teasing the businessman who was thirteen years her senior. "Digits? What is it? Nineteen ninety-nine? Do you moonlight as a rapper, too?"

"Baby girl, I'll be anything you want me to be." Chuckling, Shazir unbuttoned his suit jacket, then slid his hands into his pockets, as if he was posing for a photograph. "When are you going to let me take you out? I like a woman who plays hard to get, but don't you think this cat-and-mouse game between us has gone on long enough?"

Conflicted emotions battled inside her. Max would be pissed if he found out they were dating. Jada frowned. Or would he? Chances were he wouldn't care. He had a bevy of beauties to keep him busy, and probably never gave a second thought to what she did in her free time or whom she did it with.

"Stop playing hard to get," he admonished, checking himself out in a store window. "I'm a great guy who knows how to treat a woman right, and I guarantee we'll have fun together…"

Tempted, Jada considered his offer. She needed something to take her mind off Max, so why *not* hang out with Shazir? He was a catch, but they'd never work as a couple. He was too cocky, obviously obsessed with his physical appearance, and she suspected he spent hours in front of the mirror admiring himself. *Sure, he's not my type*, Jada conceded. *But I'm not marrying the guy; we're just having dinner!*

"Are you free tonight?"

Jada shook her head. "No, sorry. I have other plans."

It was a lie. The only plans she had were with her sofa, but Shazir didn't need to know the truth. If she accepted his last-minute invitation, he'd think she was desperate, or worse, crushing on him, and that couldn't be farther from the truth. Jada liked his personality, but she had no desire to be his girlfriend.

"Fine, then we'll hook up tomorrow after work."

Jada surprised herself by saying, "We will? What do you have in mind?"

"Dinner at Ryan Gosling's Moroccan-themed restaurant, front-row seats to see *The Nutcracker* at the Los Angeles Ballet, then cocktails at a chic lounge in Malibu."

Intrigued, Jada listened closely. Liked what he said and how he said it. She had to admit Shazir certainly had a way with words, and since Jada was a huge fan of the Los Angeles Ballet, she accepted his invitation. At his urging, she saved her number in his cell phone under the Contacts app and promised to text him later with her home address.

A car horn blared, drawing her attention to the street, and Jada spotted an elderly couple cuddling on the wooden bench in front of the bus stop. The sight gave her hope. *That's what I want, someone to grow old with who loves me for me.*

"I'll pick you up from the office. I'm working late tomorrow, so it makes more sense for me to swing by Millennium after my meeting. Can you be ready to go at five o'clock?"

Her ears perked up. She wondered how Max would feel about Shazir showing up at the office, but remembered he was going out of town tomorrow and wouldn't be back until the holiday party on Friday night. Not that it mattered. Max didn't want her, and she had to quit hoping he'd come to his senses and declare his undying love. It wasn't going to happen. Ever since the arcade, Jada had realized she'd been fooling herself. Her instincts had been wrong: they weren't a perfect match. Max wasn't attracted to her and would never be her man.

"This date is long overdue, but I hope it'll be the first of many…"

His cell phone lit up, and he trailed off speaking, staring at the device intently. Every few seconds it buzzed, and the incessant noise grated on her nerves. Jada hoped Shazir wouldn't be glued to his iPhone during dinner tomorrow night, because if he was he'd be seeing *The Nutcracker* alone. "I better go. I'll talk to you later." Eager to return to the office, Jada waved goodbye, slung her purse over her shoulder and dashed into the Vietnamese restaurant on the corner.

Minutes later, Jada left the establishment with a takeout order for Max and crossed the street. Glancing at her bracelet-style watch, she realized she'd been running errands for over an hour, and chastised herself for wasting time. If not for stopping to chitchat with Shazir, she would've already been back at the office, hard at work tackling her to-do list.

Hearing her cell ring, she glanced at the screen, hoping Max wasn't calling to check up on her. With everything going on with his dad, his clients and his employees, Max had a lot on his plate, and Jada didn't want to do anything to add to his stress. Thankful it was Taylor calling, Jada sighed in relief. She pressed the answer button, and the moment she heard the tween's voice, she knew something was wrong.

"Hi, sweetie," she greeted her, curious why Taylor was calling her in the middle of the school day. It was lunchtime, and Jada worried there was a problem at school and Taylor had been unable to reach Max at the office. "How are you? Is everything okay?"

"I need a favor."

Her voice was a whisper, so quiet that Jada strained to hear what she was saying.

"Sure, sweetie. What do you need?"

"My mom's going to Sacramento to help take care of my grandmother, which means I'm stuck going to my dad's place again this weekend."

"Taylor, that's great. Your dad loves having you around, and he always plans something fun for you guys to do, so I know you'll have a blast."

"I doubt it," she complained. "He'll be glued to his phone, working as usual, or watching football, and I'll be upstairs in my room, bored out of my mind."

Troubled by what Taylor said, Jada decided to speak to Max about his daughter's upcoming visit when she returned to the office. Taylor was changing in many different ways, and she needed her father's guidance and support now more than ever.

"I need help getting ready for the Christmas dance on Saturday night. My dad doesn't know anything about hair and makeup and I need to bring it…"

Frowning, Jada stared down at her cell. *Bring what? It's an elementary school dance!*

"Guess what? TaVonte asked me to be his date for the dance, and I said yes!" Taylor continued in a giddy, high-pitched voice. "This is my first real date, and I don't want to look like a little girl. I want to look better than T-Swift!"

Jada laughed at the tween's joke. Taylor was the spitting image of her mom, but she had her dad's sense of humor and fun-loving disposition. A bell sounded, and animated voices filled the line. Worried Taylor was going to be late for her next class and suffer her father's wrath when he found out, Jada said, "Sweetie, you should go. I'll text you later."

"Ms. Jada, can you do my hair and makeup on Saturday for the dance?"

Jada had no words, didn't know what to say in response. She didn't want to lie to Taylor, but Jada didn't think it was a good idea to hang out with the tween on the weekend, not after the conversation she'd had with Max at FunZone Galaxy. As hard as it was going to be, she had to avoid seeing her boss socially and distance herself from Taylor. If she didn't, she'd never get over Max, and would always think she had a chance with him—even though she didn't. Jada wished things could be different, but she had to protect her heart.

"Please, Ms. Jada. I won't give you any trouble. I'll be on my best behavior. I promise."

Jada adored Taylor and loved the idea of them having a girls' day, but she worried about going to her boss's estate on the weekend. What if Max was there with one of his girlfriends? How would she feel when he introduced her to his lover?

"TaVonte is the most popular boy in school, and he asked *me* to be his date for the dance. Me? Can you believe it? I know it probably doesn't seem like a big deal to you, because you probably go on dates all the time, but I'm only ten and a half, so this is *huge*."

Memories of her first school dance came to mind.

It was a disaster, one of the worst days of her life, and Jada wanted Taylor to feel confident on Saturday night, not insecure.

"Ms. Jada, are you free on Saturday?"

Stopping at the intersection, Jada leaned against the lamppost to catch her breath. She couldn't bring herself to say no to Taylor, and hoped she wouldn't regret her decision later.

"I am now!" she said with a laugh. "I'll talk to your dad first, and if it's okay with him, I'll make the necessary arrangements. We'll go shopping at the Third Street Promenade, and get our hair and nails done at one of the trendy salons. How does that sound?"

"Thank you, Ms. Jada. That would be awesome!"

"A girl never forgets her first date," she said, injecting happiness into her voice even though she felt a twinge of sadness. "It's going to be a memorable night, and I want you to look and feel your best at the Christmas dance."

"Was your first date memorable?"

Jada winced as if she had an infected tooth. "Yeah, but for all the wrong reasons."

"What happened?"

"Don't you have a class to go to?"

"Duh, it's lunchtime." Taylor giggled. "Tell me what happened at your first date."

Heat flooded Jada's skin at the thought of Valentine's Day from hell, but instead of changing the subject, she told Taylor the truth about her first school dance. "My crush was standing at the concession stand, and I was so anxious to talk to him I tripped over my feet and fell flat on my face. Everyone in the gym laughed, including my crush, and I was so embarrassed I hid out in the bathroom for the rest of the night."

The light changed, but Jada didn't move. She was

busy thinking about the worst day of her life. To this day, she couldn't look at a Valentine's Day card or heart-shaped chocolates without cringing. It had been over a decade since she'd graduated from high school, but she never forgot how her peers had made her feel inferior, as if she didn't measure up to them because of her secondhand clothes and kinky, unruly hair. Her dad never failed to tell her how beautiful she was, even when she'd had a terrible bout of acne her sophomore year, but she'd never had close friends or a boyfriend, and had always longed for a romantic relationship.

"Wow, that's savage. If that happened to me I'd have to transfer to Malibu Girls Academy, because I'd never be able to show my face at school again."

"Believe me, I tried to switch schools, but my dad wouldn't let me." Her mind transported her back to the night of the dance, and remembering how her dad had picked her up from school and taken her for ice cream made her smile. Her father meant the world to her—her siblings, too—and she'd do anything for him. "My dad told me not to let one bad day ruin my year. He was right, of course, but at the time I was crushed, and if I didn't have to help my siblings I wouldn't have left my bedroom for the rest of the year!"

Crossing the street, Jada spotted Christina North exiting Millennium Talent Agency and watched as the petite fashionista hopped into her silver SUV, then sped off. They'd met through Max, and Jada enjoyed chatting with the gregarious personal assistant to Prescott George board member Demetrius Davis. Everyone liked Christina, and handling the day-to-day bookings for the organization's Rent-a-Bachelor fund-raiser had increased her popularity.

"I found the perfect dress for the dance!" Taylor said,

changing the topic. "It's a frilly, strapless dress, with lace trim along the sides, and a…"

Listening to the tween with half an ear, Jada recalled the last telephone conversation she'd had with Christina, and still couldn't believe the scandalous things the assistant had told her about Prescott George's upper-class members. Jada had considered "booking" Max for Christmas Eve, but when she found out the staggering cost of the service she'd changed her mind. Jada couldn't think of anything better than spending the holidays with Max, but if she used all of her savings to fulfill her Christmas wish, she'd regret it when she needed emergency cash. Sure, she made great money working for Max, but she didn't have an extra five thousand dollars lying around to make her Christmas dreams come true. Her siblings needed bus passes to get to and from school, money for tuition and textbooks, and Jada wanted to help her dad with his monthly expenses.

"That sounds like a lovely dress."

"TaVonte says I look pretty in pink, and he's right. I do," she said, giggling.

Arriving at the agency, Jada said, "Sweetie, I have to go, but once I talk to your dad about Saturday I'll text you the details."

"Thanks again, Ms. Jada. You're a saint!"

Laughing at the tween's joke, she ended the call and marched into Max's spacious corner office. It was larger than her condo, and the cream furniture, polished marble floors, glass sculptures and pendant lamps gave the space a luxurious feel.

Moving quickly, Jada hung up the dry cleaning in the walk-in closet and opened the window blinds. The office had everything Max needed at his disposal—a private shower, closet and cabinet space, a mini fridge stocked with fruits, vegetables and protein shakes, and a state-of-the-art treadmill—and Max often called the office his home away from home.

Jade wiped the table and set it with silverware and napkins. Max would be back from his meeting soon, and Jada wanted everything ready and waiting by the time he returned to his office for lunch. All week, he'd been working around the clock, and Jada—

Hearing a loud, angry voice in the reception area, Jada peered through the office door, curious to see who was shouting. Millennium Talent Agency was an upscale agency that gave their celebrity clientele VIP service, and Max would be pissed if he heard one of his employees yelling and cursing in the reception area. Someone was being a nuisance, and if they didn't stop, there'd be hell to pay when the boss found out.

Jada cranked her head to the right, and her mouth dropped. She couldn't believe what she was seeing. *Max* was the nuisance, the person who was creating a scene in the reception area, and Jada feared he was having a nervous breakdown. Was he losing it? Had he finally cracked from the pressures at work, the stress of his dad's illness, the problems at Prescott George and his ongoing issues with Taylor?

Jada deliberated over what to do. Should she call 911? Or reach out to his brothers? This wasn't Max. He didn't yell or shout or curse. Ever. He was the King of Cool, the person everyone at the agency looked to during a crisis. His calm, unflappable demeanor put others at ease, especially the opposite sex, and in all the years Jada had worked for him, she'd never seen Max lose his temper.

"That no-good son of a bitch!" Huffing and puffing, Max stalked into the office and slammed the door with such force the windows rattled. "I'm going to kill him!"

Jada knew it was none of her business, and that she should return to her desk, but she was worried about Max and wanted to help. He was so handsome in a slim-fitted charcoal-gray suit that she found it hard not to stare at him. His earthy cologne was a scrumptious mix of musk, saffron and sandalwood, and her mouth watered at the scent in the air.

Max paced the length of the office. His eyebrows were furrowed, his jaw was tense, and his designer leather shoes smacked against the floor as he marched back and forth. "I have half a mind to go down to his office and kick his ass."

His gaze was wild with anger. Jada worried that if he didn't regain control he'd have a heart attack, and she couldn't imagine anything worse than seeing the man she loved collapse to the floor. "Max, what's wrong?" Hoping he'd mirror her actions, she spoke in a quiet tone of voice and remained perfectly still. "Why are you shouting?"

Balling his hands into fists, Max spoke through clenched teeth. "Because that snake Shazir Toussiant stole Kid Quentin from me!"

Chapter 8

Words didn't come. Dumbfounded, Jada stared at Max with wide eyes. She didn't understand why he was bad-mouthing his fellow Prescott George member—a man he'd known ever since he'd joined the prestigious club ten years earlier. "How is that possible?" she asked, re-claiming her voice. "Kid Quentin agreed to sign with us last week and his agent promised to fax the signed contracts back to us by Monday. It's a done deal."

"I thought so, too, but Shazir befriended the teen sen-sation online, then invited him to a party at his estate last night that included some of the biggest names in entertainment," Max explained, kicking the chocolate-brown ottoman with his foot. "The next thing I know, Kid Quentin signed with my rival, and Shazir's been bragging about it on social media."

Her temples pounded and her throat dried up. Jada couldn't speak. Didn't know what to say to make things better. She knew the two businessmen didn't like each other, but she'd never dreamed Shazir would double-cross another Prescott George member. For the second time that day, Jada had doubts about having dinner with the talent agent, and when Max cursed in Spanish she decided to text Shazir later to cancel their plans for tomorrow night. Dating him wouldn't be right. Not after what she'd learned about him. If she went out with Shazir she'd feel as if she was betraying Max, and Jada didn't want to do anything to upset her boss or jeopardize her job.

"If not for everything going on with my dad and the problems with Demetrius, I'd tell the board members at Prescott George about Shazir's dirty business practices," he said, scowling.

"Max, I'm sorry that you lost Kid Quentin."

"Me, too, and if I had a pistol I'd use it."

Surprise must have shown on her face, because Max wore an apologetic smile.

"Kid Quentin is special, and I had big plans for him." His voice was resigned, and his shoulders were hunched in defeat. "I could have mentored him and taught him the ropes about the entertainment business. He's a great kid, and we really bonded, you know?"

Moved by his confession, Jada wanted to hug him, but stayed put. Knew if she acted on her impulse it would ruin their relationship. Or worse, she'd get fired. Max spoke openly, didn't hold back how he was feeling. He wasn't upset about losing Kid Quentin as a client because of the potential financial gain; he was upset because he genuinely liked the teen and wanted to help him achieve even greater success in his career. To cheer him up, Jada wore a bright smile and spoke with confidence.

"Don't sweat it. You'll sign someone bigger and better in no time," she said, fervently nodding her head. "You're

Max Moore, talent scout extraordinaire. You don't sit around waiting for things to happen. *You* make things happen, and I have complete faith in you."

He raised his shoulders and puffed his chest out, stood taller, straighter. "Thanks, Jada. You always know just what to say to make me feel better."

His long, lingering gaze aroused her body. She could hear the phone ringing on her desk in the reception area, but Jada didn't move. How could she, when Max—her dreamy, delicious crush—was staring deep into her eyes? Her knees were knocking together like two blocks of wood, but they didn't buckle.

"You're a sweetheart, Jada, not to mention thoughtful and sincere and…"

Stepping forward, he slowly wet his lips with his tongue.

Excitement welled up inside her. *He's* finally *going to kiss me!* she thought, overcome with happiness. *Jeez, it's about time! What took him so long?*

Jada moved toward him. She closed the gap between them before she lost her nerve. She wanted Max to know she desired him more than anything, that he was the one and only man for her. The thought came out of nowhere, shocking her. Jada didn't know what was wrong with her. One minute she was determined to forget Max, and the next minute she was willing him to kiss her—and more.

It felt as if the walls were closing in around her, pushing her even closer to him, right into his arms. His lips were moving, but Jada didn't hear what he was saying, couldn't concentrate. As usual, she was too busy staring at his mouth.

Swallowing hard, Jada discreetly wiped her palms along the side of her pencil skirt. She wished she had a mint or a stick of gum to freshen her breath. She could taste a hint of garlic inside her mouth and hoped Max didn't notice. *If I'd known we were going to have our first kiss today, I wouldn't have had a vegetarian omelet for breakfast!*

Jada closed her eyes, leaned in close and waited.

And waited.

And waited.

But nothing happened. She heard the distant sound of voices, the incessant ringing of the telephone at the front desk and footsteps— Footsteps? Jada frowned. Peeling open one eye, she spotted Max sitting at his desk in his leather executive chair, and snapped to attention. He was staring at her with concern, as if he was worried about her mental state, and the expression on his face made Jada realize how stupid she'd been, how foolish. When was she going to get it through her head that he didn't want her? That she wasn't his type? The sooner she came to terms with the truth, the better off she'd be, but getting over Max was easier said than done.

"Jada, are you okay? You're not coming down with the flu, are you?" he asked, peering at her as if she was a specimen under a microscope. "I hope not, because I need you to hold down the fort when I'm in San Francisco tomorrow."

Disappointed about the kiss that wasn't, Jada forced a smile. "I will. I should get back to my desk. You still have to eat lunch, and I have tons of work to do."

Jada spun around on her heels and marched toward the door. Her feelings were all over the place, as confusing as a Shakespearean play, and it saddened her that the man she loved considered her an employee and nothing more.

"Jada, I need you to..."

His iPhone chimed, and he broke off speaking.

Facing him, she felt an overwhelming rush of emotion. On the outside, Jada was smiling, but on the inside she was struggling to keep it together. As she watched him type on his cell phone, her heart ached with sadness. He was texting a woman. Had to be. A grin covered his mouth and he looked relaxed, confident, as if he could have anything—or anyone—he wanted. And Jada didn't doubt it. Like her, most women found him irresistible.

Max erupted in laughter. "This girl," he said, typing on his cell for several seconds more.

"You were saying?" Jada prompted, scared she'd be stuck in his office for the rest of the day, forced to watch Max flirt with other women via text. "What is it you need me to do?"

He lowered his cell from his face and smiled apologetically. "Sorry about that, Jada. Taylor sent me a hilarious golf meme, and I wanted her to know I liked it. That kid. She reminds me of myself when I was that age, but *way* cooler."

"Speaking of Taylor," she began, remembering the conversation she'd had with the tween minutes earlier. "She asked if I could help her get ready for the Christmas dance on Saturday, and if it's okay with you, I was thinking we could have a girls' day out. We'll go shopping, get our hair and nails done, and have lunch at one of the trendy cafés—"

"What school dance? Taylor never mentioned it to me, and we've been texting all day."

"Then act surprised when she tells you about it," Jada said with a wry smile. "Don't spoil this for her, Max. It's a big deal, and she's over the moon about her first real date."

Jada watched the color drain from Max's face. She recognized her error, but before she could smooth things over, he complained about the planning committee at his daughter's elementary school and vowed to call the superintendent about his concerns. "Ten-year-olds shouldn't be thinking about dating. They should be thinking about their grades."

"Max, they're kids. They should have fun during the holidays, just like everyone else."

"I guess, but things were very different when I was a kid, and I'm scared my baby girl's growing up too fast. One minute she's playing with Barbies, and the next thing I know, she's gushing about some kid named TaVonte and experimenting with makeup!"

"You have nothing to worry about—"

Rap music filled the office, and Jada broke off speaking. Deciding she wasn't going to compete with an iPhone, she waited for Max to give her his undivided attention.

Max glanced down at his cell phone, but he didn't pick it up. He nodded at her to continue, as if what she had to say was important, and seemed interested in hearing her advice.

"Your daughter's a smart, spunky girl, with a fantastic personality," Jada continued. "If I had a daughter I'd want her to be just like Taylor. Don't be so hard on her. She's a great kid."

Wearing a pensive expression on his face, Max sat back in his chair and stroked his chin.

"Okay, okay, quit twisting my arm. You can take her shopping on Saturday, but keep it PG," he advised, adopting a stern voice. "Taylor has several hundred dollars on her bank card, but I don't care how much she begs and pleads—*don't* let her buy anything short, backless or see-through, and no hair extensions or fake eyelashes, either."

"Got it. You can trust me, Max. I won't let you down."

"I knew I could count on you," he said with a wink and a nod.

At his words, her heart leaped inside her chest.

"I'll pick Taylor up at breakfast and have her home by three o'clock," she explained.

"Sounds good. My brothers are coming over on Saturday afternoon, and it'll be nice to hang out with them without looking over my shoulder for Taylor. She sneaks up at me at the most inconvenient times, and thinks it's fun to scare me when I least expect it…"

Jada read between the lines. *Oh, like when you're hooking up with one of your girlfriends?*

Max snapped his fingers. "Shoot, I almost forgot. I'm flying to Maui to attend Wendell Coleman's sixtieth birthday bash after the Prescott George holiday mixer on Saturday, and I need you to buy him an expensive gift. Also, book me a suite at the Four Seasons in Maui for two nights, and reserve a rental car. Get me something fast and sexy like a Lamborghini…"

Jetting to Maui for the weekend? Now, that's *what I call the good life!* she thought, wishing she could be his plus-one for the party. Jada hated flying, but she'd conquer her fears if it meant spending the night with Max in one of the most romantic cities in the world. She'd never been on the Moore private plane, but if what her colleagues told her was true, it was the ultimate symbol of luxury and wealth, and Jada would love to see the aircraft up close.

That's not all you'd love, quipped her inner voice. *You'd do just about anything to—*

"Jada, that's all for now." Max put his cell phone to his ear, spun his chair to the window and greeted the caller on the line in Spanish.

Fluent in the language, Jada listened in on his personal call. She pursed her lips. Max was making plans to see a TV sitcom star—the one he'd dumped via text last week—and she suspected he was still romantically interested in the Mexican beauty.

Back at her desk, Jada sat down, put on her headset and logged in to her computer. She found the information for the hotel Max had requested in Maui and stared at the picturesque photographs on the hotel website.

Her cell phone lit up, and she read her newest text message. It was from Shazir. Her first thought was to delete it, but his joke brightened her mood and made a giggle tickle her throat. What was it Aubree liked to tell their single friends? Hearing her cousin's voice in her mind, she wore a wry smile. "Why stress over a man when you can just get *under* another!" the serial dater would say with a wild, boisterous laugh.

Inclining her head to the right, she gave the statement considerable thought. Gave herself a much-needed pep talk. Meeting new people was stressful, but it beat sitting at home alone every night, daydreaming about a man who didn't want her. Jada decided to take her cousin's advice. She wasn't canceling her plans with Shazir. Why should she? Max had actresses and pop stars to keep him busy, and he wouldn't care whom she hung out with after work. Her mind made up, Jada responded to Shazir's text message. She was going out with the flashy executive tomorrow, and she wasn't going to give Max a second thought.

Staring down at his cell phone, Max realized the TV sitcom star had lost her ever-loving mind, and wished he'd never hooked up with Josefina Acosta at

The Dream Hotel three months earlier. Dating her had been a mistake, one Max regretted every time the actress posted lovey-dovey messages on his social-media pages, Tweeted snarky comments to his female friends and showed up at his estate unannounced. Wanting to put an end to her incessant phone calls, text messages and emails, Max had asked Josefina to meet him for coffee, but now questioned his decision. He worried she'd make a scene at the café or do something crazy like propose. Josefina loved the paparazzi more than she loved her weekly Botox injections, and she would do anything to be the lead story on TMZ. Max didn't want to hang up on her, but if she kept talking crazy about them being "soul mates" and having a "loving, committed relationship," he'd have no choice but to end the call. Max didn't want to meet with her tonight, but knew he had to. He had to resign as her agent and make it clear that he didn't have feelings for her.

"I don't have to tell you how much this means to me," she gushed. "I adore my family, and it's important that my parents get along well with the man I love and want to marry…"

Love? Max choked on the word. *You don't love me. You love my wealth, my status and my celebrity connections, but if I lost everything tomorrow you'd be ghost!* Turned off by her speech, he allowed his mind to wander. She talked so much a telemarketer would hang up the phone on her, and Max was tempted to. Josefina wanted him to attend Christmas Day dinner at her childhood home in Guadalajara, and although he'd politely declined—twice—she continued nattering on and on about the menu, her relatives flying in from the States and the expensive Givenchy dress she'd bought on Rodeo Drive for the occasion. Her biggest flaw was that she didn't listen, and it didn't matter how many times Max told her he couldn't attend the dinner, she continued pressuring him to fly to Guadalajara on Christmas Eve.

"This year, I'm going all out for Christmas," Josefina announced. "If the Kardashians can have three Christmas trees, a vintage photo booth *and* a surprise visit from Santa, so can I!"

Bored with the conversation, Max logged in to his computer and checked his emails. He wasn't spending Christmas Day in Mexico with his former fling. It wasn't going to happen. He was spending the holidays with his family at his Santa Monica estate, and he was pulling out all the stops for the big day. He wanted Christmas with his father to be special, and it would be. His personal chef was going to prepare all of Reginald's favorite meals, and had already stocked the pantry with the best champagne and cigars money could buy.

"I have to go," Max said, anxious to get off the phone and back to work. He had scripts to read, contracts to review and sign, and dozens of emails to answer before he left for the day. "I'll meet you at Espresso & Wine Bar at six. Please don't be late. I'm going out of town tonight, so I can't stay long. One coffee, then I'm out."

"Espresso & Wine Bar?" she repeated. "That place is a dump."

Max raised an eyebrow. Not because she'd dissed his friend's coffee shop in Santa Monica, but because he could hear the disgust in her voice, the attitude. She was talking so fast he couldn't understand a word she was saying. "Excuse me?"

"You heard me. It's a three-star café with a bland

decor and menu, and I wouldn't be caught dead there. Let's go to Nobu Malibu. Celebrities flock there every night, and it's the perfect place to run into the paparazzi. I'll tip them off that we'll be in the lounge."

Max scoffed. Couldn't believe that a woman who'd been raised in a poverty-stricken neighborhood in Mexico was acting like an uptight snob born with a silver spoon in her mouth, but he ignored her disparaging comments and said, "You can do what you want, but I'm going to Espresso & Wine Bar tonight."

Josefina let out a long, dramatic sigh and spoke in a haughty tone of voice. "Fine, I'll go, but the next time we meet up you're taking me somewhere fancy and expensive."

There won't be a next time. Max said goodbye, dropped his cell on his desk and reached for the script Jada had handed him that morning when he'd arrived at the office. He needed something to take his mind off his problems, but the poorly written action flick didn't capture his attention. As he flipped to the second page his thoughts turned to his father. Life sucked. Wasn't fair. Didn't make sense. Why did Reginald have to die? Wasn't it bad enough he'd already lost his mother? Was God punishing him for his wild, bad-boy past? Max loved his glamorous lifestyle, but he'd give up everything to have more time with his father.

Wondering how Reginald was doing, he sent him a text message. They'd talked at length that morning, as Max was driving to the office, and his dad had sounded upbeat, like his old jovial self. Yesterday, when he'd worked out with his brother at Champions Boxing Gym, Trey had suggested throwing a cocktail party in Reginald's honor on Saturday night at the Prescott George headquarters, and Max had agreed. Their father's illness had brought their family closer together, and as they'd worked out side by side they'd vowed to make it a night their father would never forget. That morning, he'd mentioned his plans to Jada, and she'd agreed to book his favorite event planner, caterer and florist for the event.

Max accessed his social-media pages. He knew reading Shazir's posts would piss him off, but he couldn't resist checking up on his business rival. To his surprise, the talent agent had posted about a woman he was crushing on.

Frowning, Max scratched his head. She was probably one of his new female clients, someone young and impressionable, whom he could control. Shazir was forty years old, but he had a penchant for twenty-somethings, and the more naive, the better. Max didn't know who the woman was and didn't care. They'd been business rivals for years, but he was sick of Shazir gunning for him. The official motto of the Prescott George organization was From Generation to Generation, Lifting Each Other Up, but Shazir cared about himself and no one else, and seemed to derive great pleasure in getting under Max's skin. Got off on making him angry.

Pushing aside all thoughts of Shazir, he logged off his computer and stood. Max had more pressing matters to deal with than his problems with the ostentatious talent agent. He needed to find more evidence linking Demetrius to the sabotage case—and fast. Max wanted to clear his father's name before it was too late. It worried him to think that he'd run out of time. What bothered him more than anything was that Demetrius had lied to him weeks earlier in his home. Had looked him straight in the eye and vehemently denied setting up his best friend. But, as Max swiped his car keys and cell phone off his desk, he vowed to clear his father's name, even if it meant playing dirty.

Chapter 9

Jada stood inside the reception area of Millennium Talent Agency on Friday night, sipping her warm mulled wine, perusing the round tables covered with appetizers, desserts and cocktails. The event planner had done an outstanding job capturing the winter-wonderland theme Max wanted, and from the moment Jada arrived at the party, her colleagues had been raving about the food, the decor and the entertainment. Guests were crowded around the front desk playing Winter Charades, the line for Name That Song stretched down the hallway, and people from Human Resources were trying their luck at Blindfold Darts.

Tasting a Swedish meatball, Jada admired the extravagant decorations around the reception area. Silver snowflakes hung from the ceiling, the flickering lights from the scented candles gave the space a tranquil ambience, and snowmen decked out in red toques, scarves and sweaters were propped up against the walls. There was faux snow along the windowsill, miniature Christmas trees in every corner and edible gingerbread houses on the ledge.

Catching sight of her reflection in the wall mirror, Jada scrutinized her face. At her cousins' urging, she'd traded her eyeglasses in for a pair of contact lenses, and had been surprised by how much younger she looked without her frames. Everyone had complimented her look—except Max. He didn't notice the change, but Jada wasn't surprised. He dated centerfolds and Miss Universe types. Why would he pay *her* any mind?

Jada's cell phone vibrated inside her clutch purse, and she retrieved it from the bottom of her designer bag. Shazir's name and number popped up on the screen. She debated taking the call, knowing he'd pressure her for a second date if she did, and Jada wasn't sure if she wanted to go out with him again. They had nothing in common, and worse, he'd stolen Max's client. He'd been more interested in discussing Max than getting to know her better. His questions were endless—Had Max read any good scripts lately? Which artists was he excited about? How did he find new clients? His comments made her uncomfortable and troubled her conscience. No, there would definitely be no second date.

Jada tapped Decline, dropped her phone into her purse and tucked it under her arm. She'd touch base with Shazir later, after she left the party. He'd texted her that afternoon and invited her to accompany him to a movie premiere at Grauman's Chinese Theatre, but she'd reminded him about her office Christmas party, then politely declined his offer.

"Max, you cheated! I saw you peeking at the dartboard and I want a rematch!"

Loud voices filled the room, drowning out the Christmas music playing on the stereo system. Max, his brothers and their fiancées were obviously having fun playing Pin the Tail on Rudolph. Jada wanted to join in, but thought better of it. Didn't want to upset the close-knit group. She'd met Trey and Derek several times before, and they'd always been friendly, but Jada couldn't shake her doubts. Couldn't help feeling like she didn't belong. And she didn't. They were all successful, professional people with important careers, and she was just a lowly assistant. Would the Moore family make her feel welcome, or treat her like the outsider she was?

Doubts assailed her mind, and the weight of her insecurities overwhelmed her, making it impossible for her to move. To walk across the room and wow the Moore family with her personality. Jada scoffed at the thought. She was an average-looking woman who'd never measure up to the Beyoncés and the Rihannas of the world, and Max wasn't attracted to her. Never gave her a second glance. Deep down Jada feared she'd never find true love, and wondered if she was destined to be alone. *Will I ever meet that special someone? Will I have a loving husband and children in the future or am I just kidding myself—*

"Wow, you look great!" praised a junior talent scout, sidling up to her with a toothy grin. "It's about time you got rid of those fugly glasses and got contacts."

Jada opened her mouth to thank the Justin Timberlake look-alike for the compliment, but a male voice spoke behind her, and she broke off speaking.

"I vehemently disagree…"

As she realized who it was, a shiver snaked down Jada's spine. She glanced over her shoulder, and goose bumps flooded her skin. What was Shazir doing there? Was he trying to get her fired?

"I think your glasses make you look smart, like a sexy librarian, so get them back!"

Her lips were glued together, but she pried them apart and spoke in a calm voice. "Shazir, what are you doing here?" Jada glanced around the reception area and sighed in relief when she realized her colleagues were too busy partying to notice the impeccably dressed party crasher.

Cocking an eyebrow, he leveled a hand over the front of his slim-fitted burgundy suit jacket, then slowly licked his lips. "I'm your suave, debonair date, of course."

"I don't need a date—"

"Yes, you do," he insisted, in a firm tone of voice. "And I'm the perfect accessory."

"You have to go. This is a private function for the employees of Millennium Talent Agency, not an event open to the general public." Her legs were shaking so hard she felt unsteady on her feet, as if they were going to fall out from under her, but Jada gripped his forearm and hustled him toward the door. "Thanks for stopping by, but you have to leave."

"And miss hanging out with you? No way. Max won't mind that I'm here. We're friends."

Jada bit down on her bottom lip. She knew she shouldn't say anything about Kid Quentin, or Max's explosive temper, but she wanted Shazir gone before her boss spotted him and all hell broke loose in the reception area. "First you steal one of his favorite clients, and then you crash his office Christmas party. What do you *think* is going to happen when he sees you drinking his champagne and eating his caviar?"

"Not a damn thing. We're Prescott George members,

and squabbling in public is beneath us." Shazir winked. "Besides, I'm not here for the appetizers. I'm here for you."

The disappointment Jada felt inside must have shown on her face, because Shazir sobered quickly. Wearing an apologetic smile, he took her hand in his.

"Fine, I'll go, but you're coming with me. Let's ditch this lame party and head to the movie premiere. I want my friends and colleagues to meet the woman who's captured my heart."

Is Shazir for real? I'm not ditching my work party to watch him show off for the cameras! Dismissing his comment, she peered over his shoulder to make sure none of her coworkers were watching them. Jada noticed Alexis—the stunning fashion model who was engaged to Derek Moore—staring at them with a curious expression on her face, and hoped the mother-to-be didn't say anything to her fiancé or future brother-in-law. "I can't. I want to stay here."

"You have to be the most stubborn woman I've ever met," he complained, raking a hand through his curly jet-black hair. "What do I have to do to get through to you? To prove that I'm interested in you and want you to be my number one girl?"

It took everything in Jada not to laugh in his face. Shazir was feeding her a line. Willing to say and do anything to get his way. Reading him like a book, Jada knew what he was doing and wanted no part of it. She wasn't going to let him use her to get under Max's skin, and made up her mind to delete his number from her cell phone once he left the party. He wasn't worth her time, and she had no desire to date the flashy talent agent with a massive ego.

"Please leave," she implored, desperate to get through

to him. Time was of the essence, and if she didn't make Shazir understand the severity of the situation, there could be serious consequences for them both. "If Max sees you he'll lose it, and I don't want to upset him."

A sneer curled his lips. "But I do."

"I won!" Max ripped off his blindfold and stalked toward the laminated picture of Rudolph the Red-Nosed Reindeer taped to the wall. He raised his arms triumphantly in the air. Max knew it was wrong to gloat, but he couldn't resist celebrating his come-from-behind victory over his brothers. "I told you guys I'd win, but you didn't believe me. Said I was all talk and no action," he reminded them, cocking an eyebrow. "Well, how ya like me now, boys?"

His brothers chuckled, their fiancées did, too, and the sound of their boisterous laughter bolstered his mood. Made Max momentarily forget his problems. His business trip to San Francisco had been a bust. He'd decided not to sign the boy band, or the aspiring actress he'd been in talks with for weeks. He didn't think they had the "It" factor, and the only bright spot of his two-day trip had been shopping for Taylor. He'd bought everything on her Christmas list, and couldn't wait to see the look on his daughter's face when she opened her presents on Christmas Day.

"I thought I was competitive," Trey said, "but, Max, you're on a whole *other* level."

Max shrugged. "Guilty as charged. What can I say? I hate to lose."

Kiara's ponytail swished back and forth as she nodded her head. "You're not the only one. I beat Trey at Scrabble and he pouted for an entire week! After that, I just let him win."

Chuckling, Max grabbed his tumbler off the table and finished his candy cane vodka. He enjoyed having his family around, and was glad his brothers and their wives-to-be had agreed to attend his office holiday party.

"I should have known. I knew I was good at Scrabble, but not *that* good." Trey wrapped Kiara up in his arms. "I know how much you love this song, so let's dance."

"Let It Snow" was playing on the stereo system, and Trey belted out the lyrics as he slow-danced with his fiancée. Max felt his eyes bug out of his head. His brother's behavior was shocking. That wasn't Trey. He was an award-winning screenwriter, not an aspiring singer. His brother didn't fawn over women, but watching Trey with Kiara proved he was completely devoted to the businesswoman with the dazzling smile.

"It's time to pay up, so quit stalling." Max stuck out his hand and wiggled his fingers. "I beat you fair and square, and now I want my kizzash."

Derek reached into the back pocket of his charcoal-gray dress pants, took out his leather wallet and opened it. Scowling, he fished out five hundred-dollar bills, slapped them into the palm of Max's hand and said, "There. Happy now?"

"Thanks, bro! It was great doing business with you." Max closed his eyes and fanned his face with the crisp bills. "*Man*, this feels good. You should try it sometime."

"I'm glad you won," Derek said. "Now that you have some money you can go buy yourself some class because you're the worst trash-talker I've ever met."

Max shrugged. "Don't blame me. Blame Dad. He taught me everything I know!"

Alexis winced as if in pain, then exhaled a deep breath.

"Alexis, what's wrong?" Sobering, Max pocketed his winnings and studied his future sister-in-law closely. He remembered how sick Shay had been when she'd been pregnant with Taylor, and hoped Alexis didn't have complications, too. "Everything okay with my nephew?"

An amused expression covered her face. "Your *nephew*?"

"What makes you so sure we're having a boy? There could be a little girl in here, for all you know," Derek joked, reaching out to touch his fiancée's flat stomach. Early in her first trimester, Alexis wasn't sporting a baby bump yet, and still hadn't told any of her friends.

Raising his glass to his mouth, Max nodded in agreement. "Just a lucky guess, but it doesn't matter to me what gender the baby is. I'm going to spoil them rotten, and you can't stop me."

"Is that Jada in the gold sweater dress? I almost didn't recognize her without her glasses."

Mad at himself for not realizing it sooner, Max shook his head. He knew there was something different about her when he'd breezed past her desk that afternoon after returning from his trip, but he was on his cell. Max wished he'd stopped to tell Jada how pretty she looked. Blessed with a slender, curvy body, Jada was humble about her beauty, which made her even more attractive to the opposite sex. Several of his male employees were romantically interested in her, but Max had made it clear from day one that Jada was off-limits.

Damn, Max thought, raising his glass to his mouth. Had her eyes always been luminous and bright and impossible to look away from? And if so, why hadn't he noticed before?

That's what you get for not paying attention, chided his inner voice. *If you had put away your cell instead of responding to Josefina's angry text messages, you would have noticed Jada was wearing contacts, not glasses, and a fitted designer dress.*

"I didn't know Jada and Shazir were a couple," Trey continued. "When did they hook up?"

Max choked on the ice cube in his mouth. *What?* The words blared in his thoughts, and for a moment he couldn't think or speak. Lost all use of his tongue and the ability to form sentences.

Bewildered by his brother's words, Max blinked, then noticed the talent agent with the bad-boy reputation was standing beside his assistant. He'd been so busy admiring Jada he'd failed to notice Shazir gazing at her with lust in his beady little eyes.

Gripping his tumbler, he wished it was the executive's neck. What was he doing here? Who invited him? His thoughts spun. Was he with Jada? Max couldn't understand why Jada—a smart, sensible woman—would want to date the fortysomething bachelor. Sure, Shazir was attractive in a cheesy, boy-band-member kind of way, but he was arrogant as hell, and he didn't have an honest bone in his body.

Searching for answers, his mind raced from one thought to the next. Shazir was standing so close to her Max would need a crowbar to separate them, but what bothered him more than anything was the broad I'm-the-man grin on the executive's face. They were lovers? Why?

"They make a cute couple," Kiara said. "And you can tell by Shazir's goofy, lopsided smile that he's totally into her. He looks happier than a kid at a Pokémon Convention!"

Max slammed his empty glass on the table. "I'll be right back."

Derek clapped a hand on Max's shoulder, and Trey slid in front of him, blocking his path.

"Don't do anything stupid," Trey advised, adopting a stern tone of voice. "This is a party, not Champions Boxing Gym, and if you start a fight with Shazir, it could have serious consequences for all of us, including Dad."

"And the last thing we need is more drama. We have enough on our plate as it is," Derek added.

"Who's fighting?" Max asked, cracking his knuckles. "I just want to talk to the guy."

Derek nodded. "Fine, then we'll come with you."

Annoyed that he suddenly had two chaperones, Max crossed the room, rehearsing in his mind what he wanted to say to his brown-eyed nemesis. Should he curse Shazir out for stealing Kid Quentin from under his nose or play it cool, not give him the satisfaction of seeing him sweat? Deciding the latter was the way to go, Max clapped Shazir hard on the back and thanked him for coming to the party. "It's good to see you," he lied, his smile as fake as a three-dollar bill. "I'm glad you could join us tonight."

"See, baby, I told you Max wouldn't mind me stopping by." Oozing with confidence and pride, Shazir slid an arm around Jada's waist and rubbed her hips. "Jada told me you were upset that Kid Quentin dropped you so he could sign with my agency…"

She. Said. What? Max stared at Jada with wide eyes. He couldn't believe she'd blabbed to the competition about their private conversation in his office days earlier, and figured Shazir was lying, just trying to get under his skin. But when Jada dropped her gaze to the floor, Max knew she'd betrayed his trust.

"Jada said you wouldn't want me here, but I assured her it was water under the bridge."

Water under the bridge? Max thought, inwardly fuming. *It happened two days ago, you low-down dirty snake! And Jada's right, you creep; I* don't *want you here, so leave!*

Trey cleared his throat. He must have sensed Max's rage, because he stepped forward, shielding Shazir with his body and wisely changing the subject. "Are you free tomorrow night? We're having a holiday mixer at Prescott George for our dad, and all members are welcome."

"I'll let you know. I don't know if you've heard, but I'm the star of the Rent-a-Bachelor campaign. I've single-handedly raised more money than any of the other members, and I'm booked solid until Christmas Eve," he bragged, popping the collar on his white dress shirt.

"Then what are you doing here?" Max cocked an eyebrow. "Shouldn't you be at a five-star restaurant wining and dining one of your dates?"

"Jada begged me to come tonight, and I didn't have the heart to disappoint her."

Max scoffed. Didn't believe a word he said. He watched Shazir flirt with Jada and felt such a strong sense of betrayal it rocked him to the core. He'd seen enough. Couldn't stand to be around Shazir another second and feared if he didn't leave he'd slug him in the face. "If you'll excuse us, I need to have a word with my assistant," Max said, stepping forward.

"Okay, but bring her right back." Licking his lips, he let his gaze slide down Jada's fine feminine shape.

"She promised me a dance, and I've been looking forward to it all day."

"See you around, Shazir. Have fun at *my* party."

The grin slid off Shazir's mouth, and a sneer darkened his face. "If Jada's not back here in five minutes I'm coming to get her, got it?"

Ignoring him, Max took Jada by the arm and led her through the reception area and into the conference room. It was empty, but there were dirty plates and Christmas-themed bowls filled with caramel popcorn on the table. Releasing her, Max stared her down. "You had no right to discuss our private conversation with your lover."

"Shazir isn't my lover—"

Relief flowed through his body, and his arms dropped to his sides. "He's not? Then why did he have his hands all over you? Why is he here?"

"Max, I didn't invite him. He showed up unannounced and I was trying to get rid of him, so I told him you were pissed about the Kid Quentin deal, hoping he'd leave, but he didn't."

"I don't want Shazir knowing my private business," he continued. "What happens at *my* agency stays at *my* agency. Understood?"

"Absolutely. It won't happen again. I promise."

Her apologetic smile softened his heart. He felt guilty for ever doubting her loyalty, and wished he'd kept his cool back in the reception area. "Do you love him?"

"Who? Shazir? Don't be silly. I hardly know the guy. We've only been on one date."

Max raked a hand through his hair. It was none of his business whom Jada dated or what she did in her free time, but he couldn't stop himself from asking the question in the forefront of his mind. "Are you lovers? Did you sleep with him?"

"No, and I don't plan to. Shazir's a lot of fun, and he tells great stories, but he's not my type." Jada grabbed a handful of popcorn, tossed one into her mouth and gestured to the door with a nod of her head. "I should get back to the party before Shazir starts a conga line. He said every event needs a signature dance, but I fervently disagreed."

"He's right, but make sure it's not the 'Nae Nae.' I hate that dance!" Jada laughed, and Max did, too. Glad she wasn't mad at him for losing his temper, he thanked her for planning a great office party and chuckled when she asked for a raise. One minute they were cracking jokes, and the next thing Max knew, they were pressed against each other, kissing as if it was the most natural thing in the world. His mind was screaming, "No!" but his body was screaming, "Yes!"

Her lips were sweet, flavored with caramel and addictive. They were intoxicating, the best thing that had ever happened to his mouth since bourbon-flavored cigars. Her perfume was floral and fruity, a subtle feminine scent that tickled his nostrils. Max told himself to stop, that he was making a mistake, but he wanted Jada and wasn't going to deprive himself the pleasure of her kiss. He'd never had romantic feelings for an employee, but he was helpless to resist her. Jada pulled away, but Max tightened his hold around her waist.

Max could hear laughter, conversation and music in the distance, but their moans and groans drowned out the noises of the party. Electricity coursed between them, crackled like lightning. Max imagined himself picking Jada up, putting her down on the table and hiking her legs in the air. He wanted to bury himself deep inside her, could almost see it now. Max couldn't control his thoughts or his wayward hands. He caressed her shoulders, rubbed and stroked her hips. Desperate for her, he cupped her face in his hands and backed her up against the door. When Jada slid her tongue into his mouth and teased his tongue with her own, chills rocked his horny body. Later, when Max told his brothers what happened in the conference room with Jada, he'd have no recollection of who made the first move, but he'd remember how incredible it had been kissing her. He'd never entertained the idea of them hooking up before, but he couldn't deny their sexual chemistry and how much he enjoyed holding her close to his chest.

Someone pounded on the door, then wiggled the knob. Jada jumped back, out of his arms, and Max strangled a groan. It had to be Shazir looking for Jada and Max was pissed about the interruption. Damn him! Why couldn't the pretty boy find someone else? Why did he have his sights set on Jada? The doorknob stopped shaking, and then footsteps echoed in the corridor. Max stared at Jada, couldn't take his eyes off her. He saw her quick intake of breath, the dazed expression on her face, and wondered what she was thinking.

"I shouldn't have kissed you," he admitted, concerned about the fallout from his behavior. He wasn't afraid of her contacting HR or suing him for sexual harassment; he was worried about her quitting. She was the best assistant he'd ever had, and he didn't want to lose her. "Jada, I'm sorry. I don't know what got into me, but I assure you it won't happen again."

Sadness flickered in her eyes, but she nodded her head, as if she wholeheartedly agreed with his statement. "I understand," she said quietly, fiddling with the silver bracelet on her left wrist. "Alcohol makes people do crazy things sometimes."

Yeah, that's true, but I'm stone-cold sober, he thought, staring at her lush mouth. He wished her lips and her curvy body were still pressed against his, but wisely kept his distance.

"Good night, Max. Enjoy the rest of the party." Jada unlocked the door then yanked it open. "I'll be by around noon to pick up Taylor, so see you tomorrow."

Max stepped forward, found himself following her into the darkened corridor like a lost puppy looking for a home. He didn't want Jada to leave with Shazir; he wanted her to leave with him, but when he opened his mouth to confess the truth the words didn't come.

Chapter 10

The blue-eyed stylist in the striped keyhole dress at Luxe Beauty Salon spun Jada's chair around with a dramatic flourish and pointed at the beveled mirror in front of her workstation. "I hope you like the sleek, eye-framing cut. It's the latest hair trend, and *très* chic."

A gasp escaped Jada's mouth. She almost didn't recognize herself, couldn't believe the image staring back at her. Arriving at the salon with Taylor two hours earlier, she'd asked the stylist to make her look sexy but smart, to give her a hairstyle befitting the assistant to a major talent agent, and the brunette had delivered. *Is that* really *me?*

Leaning forward in her seat, Jada studied her reflection for several seconds. *Wow!* echoed in her mind. Her hair had been colored, washed and trimmed, but she'd been so busy reading magazines she hadn't noticed what the stylist was doing. Her transformation was jaw-dropping, and Jada loved everything about it. Long, sweeping bangs were draped dramatically over one eye, and curls cascaded down her shoulders, giving her a youthful look. Best of all, her hair looked vibrant and healthy.

Turning her head from right to left, Jada assessed every angle. Goodbye, dull, boring brown, and hello, radiant honey-blond highlights! She wanted to dance around the salon, but resisted the urge. Didn't want to embarrass herself or Taylor, who was sitting in the chair beside hers reading a graphic novel. Jada couldn't remember the last time she'd been this excited—

Of course you do, challenged her inner voice. *Last night when you kissed Max!*

Jada tried not to think about that kiss, the one that stole her breath, but she couldn't control her thoughts. Alone with Max in the conference room, she'd fallen under his spell, and when he'd swept her up into his arms and pressed his mouth against hers she'd collapsed against his chest. It was the moment she'd been waiting two long years for, and the kiss did not disappoint.

An image of Max filled her mind, and Jada licked her lips. Sensual, passionate and hot, the kiss was everything she'd hoped it would be. She'd never experienced anything like it. Jada only wished it had happened at his estate rather than the office conference room, because there was no doubt in her mind that if they'd been alone at his waterfront mansion, they would have made love. Jada wanted Max to be her first, and hoped when the time came he wouldn't get cold feet. Or worse, reject her. Her ex-boyfriend had freaked out the night she told him the truth—which she didn't like thinking about—and Jada was scared history would repeat itself. Painful memories came rushing back, stealing her joy, but she pushed

"FAST FIVE" READER SURVEY

Your participation entitles you to:
✳ 4 Thank-You Gifts Worth Over $20!

Complete the survey in minutes.

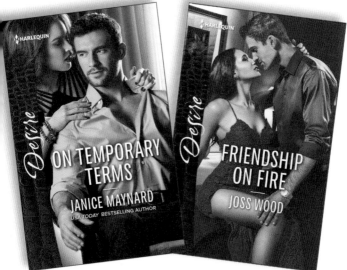

Get **2 FREE Books**

See inside for details.

Dear Reader,

Since you are a lover of our books, your opinions are important to us... and so is your time.

That's why we made sure your **"FAST FIVE" READER SURVEY** can be completed in just a few minutes. Your answers to the five questions will help us remain at the forefront of women's fiction.

And, as a thank-you for participating, we'd like to send you **4 FREE THANK-YOU GIFTS!**

Enjoy your gifts with our appreciation,

Pam Powers

To get your
4 FREE THANK-YOU GIFTS:

✳ Quickly complete the "Fast Five" Reader Survey
and return the insert.

"FAST FIVE" READER SURVEY

1	Do you sometimes read a book a second or third time?	○ Yes ○ No
2	Do you often choose reading over other forms of entertainment such as television?	○ Yes ○ No
3	When you were a child, did someone regularly read aloud to you?	○ Yes ○ No
4	Do you sometimes take a book with you when you travel outside the home?	○ Yes ○ No
5	In addition to books, do you regularly read newspapers and magazines?	○ Yes ○ No

YES! I have completed the above Reader Survey. Please send me my 4 FREE GIFTS (gifts worth over $20 retail). I understand that I am under no obligation to buy anything, as explained on the back of this card.

225/326 HDL GM3T

FIRST NAME   LAST NAME

ADDRESS

APT.#   CITY

STATE/PROV.   ZIP/POSTAL CODE

READER SERVICE—Here's how it works:

Accepting your 2 free Harlequin Desire® books and 2 free gifts (gifts valued at approximately $10.00 retail) places you under no obligation to buy anything. You may keep the books and gifts and return the shipping statement marked "cancel." If you do not cancel, about a month later we'll send you 6 additional books and bill you just $4.55 each in the U.S. or $5.24 each in Canada. That is a savings of at least 13% off the cover price. It's quite a bargain! Shipping and handling is just 50¢ per book in the U.S. and 75¢ per book in Canada*. You may cancel at any time, but if you choose to continue, every month we'll send you 6 more books, which you may either purchase at the discount price plus shipping and handling or return to us and cancel your subscription. *Terms and prices subject to change without notice. Prices do not include applicable taxes. Sales tax applicable in N.Y. Canadian residents will be charged applicable taxes. Offer not valid in Quebec. Books received may not be as shown. All orders subject to approval. Credit or debit balances in a customer's account(s) may be offset by any other outstanding balance owed by or to the customer. Please allow 4 to 6 weeks for delivery. Offer available while quantities last.

▲ If offer card is missing write to: Reader Service, P.O. Box 1341, Buffalo, NY 14240-8531 or visit www.ReaderService.com ▲

BUSINESS REPLY MAIL
FIRST-CLASS MAIL   PERMIT NO. 717   BUFFALO, NY

POSTAGE WILL BE PAID BY ADDRESSEE

READER SERVICE
PO BOX 1341
BUFFALO NY 14240-8571

NO POSTAGE
NECESSARY
IF MAILED
IN THE
UNITED STATES

them aside. She refused to let anything ruin her girls' day with Taylor.

"Jada, dear, what's wrong?" the stylist asked, a concerned expression on her heart-shaped face. "Why are you frowning? You're not feeling your fabulous new hairstyle?"

Blinking, she surfaced from her thoughts. "No, it's great. Thank you so much."

Taylor snapped her fingers in the air. "Get it, Ms. Jada! You look incredible."

"Thanks, sweetie. It's different, but I love it. It's exactly what I wanted."

"My dad's going to love it, too. He likes women with long, curly hair."

Jada raised an eyebrow. Taken aback by the tween's words, she wondered what the fifth grader was up to. All day, Taylor had been making comments about her dad's personal life—*he doesn't like women who curse... he won't date someone who smokes...he falls hard for females he can have smart, intelligent conversation with*—and although Jada changed the subject every time Taylor mentioned her father's "ideal type," she couldn't help feeling guilty for taking mental notes and storing the information about Max in the back of her mind.

The salon, filled with dozens of attractive women wearing the latest fashions, was buzzing with conversation, but the male stylist flat-ironing Taylor's hair gave Jada a toothy smile. "I want to see you again," he announced, vigorously nodding his head, his thick black curls tumbling around his forehead. "So, slide me your number so we can make it happen."

Stunned by how bold he was, Jada stared at him with wide eyes. *Is he for real, or is he pulling my leg?* Cute, with dark features and a lanky frame, he'd been making her laugh ever since she'd arrived at the salon. And if she wasn't crushing on Max, she'd take the Colombian native up on his offer. Jada loved dancing, and often joked that she could beat J-Lo in a dance battle, but she wanted Max to be her dance partner, not the flirtatious stylist.

"Sorry, Gerardo, she's busy," Taylor quipped with a cheeky smile, dropping her graphic novel in her lap. "Better luck next time, *papi*!"

Cracking up, the stylist wagged his finger at the tween. "Good one, *bebita*."

Giving Taylor a grateful smile, Jada flashed her a thumbs-up. The fifth grader wasn't a good girl, she was a *great* girl, and Jada loved spending time with her. Bright and early that morning, she'd driven the forty-five minutes to Max's waterfront estate. Although she'd been nervous about seeing him after their sizzling kiss last night, she'd wiped her damp palms along the side of her skinny jeans, knocked on the front door and greeted Max with an easy-breezy smile. He'd waved her inside, and his calm, cool demeanor had instantly put her at ease. Inside the foyer, Max had given Taylor a stern talking-to about being on her best behavior then excused himself to take a phone call. Or perhaps to avoid speaking to Jada about that explosive kiss that made her temperature soar.

In the car, Taylor had been busy on her cell phone, texting, Tweeting and scrolling, but when they arrived at the Third Street Promenade, she'd linked arms with Jada and dragged her into her favorite clothing store. The upscale shopping, dining and entertainment complex in downtown Santa Monica was only steps away from the Pacific Ocean. With everything from farmers-market produce to designer fashions and electronics, the open-air promenade was a shopper's nirvana, and a hit among locals and tourists alike. Lively street performers and musicians had created a festive mood. The streets were noisy, chock-full of holiday shoppers searching for the perfect Christmas gift, but Jada and Taylor had had fun strolling around the promenade, enjoying the sights and sounds around them. They'd found dresses, accessories and shoes in a popular department store, then had lunch at a burger restaurant famous for its fresh ingredients, homemade sauces and signature drinks. Seated on the patio, eating their entrées, they'd chatted about their families, their favorite Christmas songs and movies, and their celebrity crushes.

"Gerardo, thank you, thank you, thank you!" Taylor shouted, dancing around in her leather swivel chair. "I look prettier than Zendaya!"

Giggling, the tween stroked her lush, silky locks, then whipped her hair back and forth. Taylor blew herself a kiss in the mirror and everyone standing nearby burst out laughing.

"Do you think TaVonte's going to like my hair?" Taylor asked.

"Of course he will, but what matters most is what *you* think. Do you like it?"

Nodding, she scooped her cell phone out of her lap and snapped a selfie.

"Ms. Jada, can I get my makeup professionally done, too? *Please?*" she begged, clasping her hands together. "I've always wanted extra-long eyelashes and glitter lipstick. All my classmates have it done, and it looks *so* cool."

Jada shook her head. She didn't need to think about it, even though the tween had a desperate look on her face. "If you go home with makeup your dad will kill me, and I'm too young to die!"

"One o'clock mani-pedis for Taylor Moore and Jada Allen?" asked a female voice.

"That's us," Taylor said, waving her hands wildly in the air. "We're here!"

"Wonderful. Are you lovely ladies ready to be thoroughly spoiled and pampered?"

Taylor leaped off her chair as if it was on fire, and cheered. "I was born ready!"

Ten minutes later, Jada was soaking her feet in a tub of salt water, sipping a complimentary glass of sparkling lemonade. Everything about the VIP lounge was relaxing—the sky murals painted on the ivory ceiling, the stunning array of potted plants and exotic flowers, and the dim lights. Jada finished her drink, put the empty glass on the side table and closed her eyes. Took a moment to reflect on the day, and how much fun she was having with Taylor.

The air smelled of scented oils, the instrumental jazz music playing in the salon was calming, and the ten-minute hand and foot massage by the technician was heaven. All her stress left her body, and for the first time in months, Jada felt confident, as if she could tackle every hurdle, every challenge, including her feelings for Max. And she wasn't going to wait until Monday to talk to him; she was going to speak to him when she dropped Taylor home. At the thought, every muscle in her body clenched, but it was high time she came clean to Max, and the sooner, the better.

"Ms. Jada, do you like my dad?"

Her eyes flew open. Convinced she'd misheard the question, Jada cranked her head to the right. Before she could gather her thoughts, Taylor spoke, and the fifth grader's boldness blew Jada's mind, proved she was definitely Max Moore's daughter.

"Come on," she urged. "Answer the question. Do you like my dad or not?"

"Of course I do. He's my boss, and we've worked well together for many years."

"No, I mean in a romantic way. Like the way I feel about TaVonte."

A lie fell from her lips. "No, of course not. I'm, ah, dating someone."

"That's too bad. I know my dad can be salty sometimes, but you're definitely his favorite staff."

"I am?" Jada asked, unable to hide her surprise. "Who told you that?"

"My dad, of course. He talks about you nonstop." Taylor affected a deep, masculine voice. "'I'll ask Jada. She knows everything... Jada's an outstanding employee, and I don't know what I would do without her... Jada's the *real* star of the agency, and I'm lucky to have her.'"

Jada read the situation perfectly and asked the fifth grader the question running through her mind. "Taylor, are you trying to find a girlfriend for your dad?"

"I sure am. If he's booed up he'll stop bothering me."

Smiling, Jada reached out and patted her hand. "He's your dad, Taylor. That's his job."

"But he treats me like a baby, and he never listens to me. It's annoying, Ms. Jada."

"I know, but in his eyes you'll always be his baby girl, and that will never change."

"Oh, brother." Sighing deeply, as if she had the cares of the world on her shoulders, Taylor fiddled with the silver mood ring on her left thumb. "Now I'm *really* depressed."

"Don't be. That's just the way dads are. I'm twenty-seven, and my dad *still* calls to check up on me three or four times a day. He reminds me to eat healthy, to set my home alarm at night, and threatens to beat up anyone who upsets me."

Her eyes widened. "Really? But you're an adult."

"I know, and I wish someone would tell my dad that!" Laughing, Jada thought about the conversation she'd had that morning with Ezekiel as she was driving to Malibu. "To be honest, it's kind of sweet. It doesn't matter how old you get, you'll always have your dad's love and support."

"I never looked at it that way."

"You should, and trust me, you could have it much worse," she pointed out.

"I can't think of anything worse than my dad treating me like a baby, especially in front of my friends. It's the worst!"

"My uncle Harrison was a drag queen, and when I was a kid, every day he'd pick up my cousin Aubree from school in a ridiculously long wig and silk Chanel pajamas—"

"OMG! I'd die of embarrassment if my dad did something like that!" Taylor shivered, then rubbed her hands along the arms of her cropped knit sweater. "TaVonte lives with his grandparents, and he's always telling me how lucky I am to have a dad who loves me."

"He's a very wise young man, Taylor. You should listen to him."

A cell phone buzzed, and Taylor and Jada both reached for their iPhones.

Hoping she had a message from Max, Jada punched in her password. She'd texted him at lunch, to let him know how Taylor was doing, but he hadn't responded. That was unlike him. He always answered her texts promptly, and she worried about what his silence meant.

When she saw that her phone had pinged with a text

from Shazir, not Max, her throat closed up and went so dry she couldn't swallow. Did Max regret their passionate, no-holds-barred kiss last night? Had he already moved on to someone else? Did he have female company at his estate? Was that why Max hadn't replied to her message? Because he was—

Jada slammed the brakes on her thoughts, refused to think the worst about him. His divorce had soured his opinion of relationships, but he was a catch, the kind of man she'd be proud to take home to her family in Inglewood, and all she wanted for Christmas was Max. She wanted to know if the kiss meant anything to him, and although she was nervous about asking him point-blank, she needed to know the truth. Frowning, she read Shazir's message.

I want you to be my date for the Prescott George holiday mixer tonight. I have something important to talk to you about, so I'll pick you up from your condo at six.

Taking a moment to consider his invitation, Jada tapped her index finger against her cell phone case. She suspected Shazir was using her to get under Max's skin, and wanted no part of his deception. Days earlier, Max had invited her to the cocktail party they were throwing in his dad's honor at the Prescott George headquarters, and Jada had agreed to go. Reginald had a larger-than-life personality, and Jada loved hearing his hilarious childhood stories about Max. Could listen to him talk for hours about his mischievous son—and all the trouble he used to cause at his exclusive Brentwood private school. Before she could text Shazir back, another message from him popped up on her screen.

I have a life-changing business proposition for you that could take your career to the next level, and fatten your bank account. See you at six, Beautiful, and wear something short, red and sexy!

A life-changing business proposition? What is that about? And why is Shazir being vague? Doubts plagued her thoughts. Just then, Taylor spoke, and her loud, bubbly voice captured Jada's attention. Deciding to call Shazir later, she dropped her cell in her purse and faced the tween.

"I'm so excited about the dance I wish I was already there!"

"I bet," Jada said with a laugh. "I hope you enjoy every minute of it."

"I will. To be honest, it's all I can think about." Giggling, Taylor flipped her smooth, silky hair over her shoulders. "There's a lake near my school, and yesterday when TaVonte and I were eating lunch at our favorite bench, he promised to bring me flowers tonight. I can't wait."

Seated side by side, watching the nail technicians work, Jada and Taylor discussed gift ideas for their friends and family, and skating at the holiday ice rink in Santa Monica in the coming weeks. In good spirits, Taylor spoke about her best friends at school, her extra-curricular activities and how cool her mom was. When she joked about her dad being a "grumpy old man," Jada spoke up, unable to let the disparaging comment slide. She asked Taylor to be more respectful of her dad, and after an awkward silence, the tween promised she would.

Three hours after arriving at the salon, Jada paid the bill, thanked the staff for their help and ushered Taylor out the front door. The streets were so crowded it was hard to walk. Police officers in orange helmets patrolled the area on bicycles, tourists with selfie sticks posed for pictures all across the promenade, and panhandlers begged for change. Pressed for time, Jada suggested they get ice cream another day, but Taylor poked out her bottom lip and Jada caved like a house of cards. "Okay, we'll stop at Creams and Dreams, but you have to make it quick."

The girl's eyes were brighter than the sun. "Thanks, Ms. Jada. My dad was right. You *are* the best."

"Has anyone ever told you that you're exactly like him?"

"Grandma Virginia says it all the time, but I try not to hold it against her."

Laughing, they strode into the ice-cream parlor and joined the line. While Taylor placed her order with the shop clerk, Jada checked her cell phone for missed calls. Nothing. Still no response from Max. At the thought of him, her pulse sped up. Jada was excited about showing off her new look and hoped she'd be confident, not nervous, when they spoke about their relationship. Max was the one Jada wanted, the man of her dreams, and tonight she was ready to put her heart on the line.

Chapter 11

"Turn it off. I've seen enough." Pushing away from the round table inside Max's gourmet kitchen, Derek jumped to his feet. Pacing in front of the windows, he mumbled under his breath about being emotionally scarred and needing a shot of whiskey. His head bent, he stuffed his hands into the pockets of his faded blue jeans, cursing the midwife who'd posted the natural childbirth video online. "I can't watch anymore. It's too disturbing."

Max chuckled. "Man up, D. We haven't even gotten to the good part yet. Wait until the baby's head crowns. There's nothing quite like it."

Derek shivered, as if he was standing naked inside a skating rink, then pressed his eyes shut. "I don't know why I let you guys talk me into watching that stupid video," he complained. "How am I supposed to sleep tonight after seeing childbirth up close and personal?"

Trey scoffed. "It's nothing you haven't seen before.

You've hooked up with more women than an NBA player, and you brag about it every time we play poker!"

"Yeah, well, that was before I reunited with Alexis. Now that I have my girl, I don't need anyone else, and I don't want to watch any more gruesome videos, so get rid of it."

Max scoffed. "It's a childbirth video, D, not a horror movie!"

"It might as well be," Derek grumbled, leaning against the granite breakfast bar. "I wish I'd plugged my ears when the mother collapsed on the bed, screaming bloody murder. I'll never get that sound out of my mind, and it's all your fault, Max. Thanks a lot."

"Quit whining. You haven't seen nothing yet." Max picked up his beer and tasted it.

"And I don't plan to." Derek stuck out his thumb and rattled off his list of duties when Alexis was admitted to the hospital. "I'm in charge of feeding Alexis ice chips, rubbing her back and taking pictures once the baby is born, and that's it."

"Come on, man. You have to cut the umbilical cord. It's your duty as a father."

"I… I—I don't think I can," Derek stammered, tugging at the collar of his tan lightweight sweater. "And I don't want anything to do with the afterbirth, either. I overheard Alexis on the phone yesterday, and her great-grandmother advised her to take the placenta home and plant it in the backyard. Says it's supposed to bring good luck."

"Ah, hell, naw!" Trey scrunched up his nose. "That's just nasty!"

Derek sighed. "Finally. Now you guys understand what I'm going through."

"And it only gets worse from here," Max said with a

wry smile. His thoughts returned to that morning, and he reflected on the argument he'd had with Taylor after breakfast. Busy watching videos on her cell phone, she'd refused to clean her room, and when Max had threatened to ground her for a month, she'd stomped upstairs and slammed her bedroom door. "Like women, kids are ungrateful, impossible to please and never satisfied."

"Speak for yourself. Kiara's an angel," Trey bragged with a broad, toothy smile. "She's the best thing that's ever happened to me, and if I had my way we'd already be married."

"Alexis is a gracious, compassionate soul, and I have absolutely no complaints." Derek's face softened. "I've met a lot of females, but no one compares to Alexis. She's my heart, my everything, the wind beneath my wings…"

An image of Jada popped in Max's mind, and his heart skipped a beat. Thundered in his ears. There was no denying it. No escaping the truth. Max was taken with her. Attracted to her. Wanted to make love to her in every sexual position imaginable.

Aroused by the explicit thought, his mouth dried, and an erection rose inside his cargo pants, stabbing his zipper. How was that even possible? Max wondered, racking his brain for answers. He'd never once given her a second glance, so why was he lusting after her now? Craving her mouth? Itching to stroke her curves? All day, he'd thought about that kiss, and nothing else. Couldn't concentrate long enough to read contracts or movie scripts, and if his brothers hadn't stopped by to discuss the San Diego chapter's sabotage case, Max would still be in his home office, reliving the moment he'd kissed Jada at the office Christmas party. He'd never experienced anything like it. The kiss was passionate, packed with lust and heat, arousing every inch of his body.

Questions crowded his mind. Was he romantically interested in Jada because they had an undeniable connection, or because Shazir was pursuing her? Sitting back comfortably in his chair, he considered the executive's motives. Shazir was a wolf in sheep's clothing, the kind of man who'd do anything to lure a woman into bed, and Max didn't want to see Jada get hurt. She deserved to be with someone who would cherish her. And although he'd never admit it to anyone, not even himself, Max wanted to be that person—at least during the Christmas holidays.

A cell phone rang, filling the kitchen with hip-hop music, and Derek excused himself from the table to take the call. Glancing at the flat-screen TV mounted to the wall, Trey chuckled at the sportscaster's joke, then vigorously nodded his head in agreement. "I couldn't have said it better myself." Trey grabbed a handful of chips from the plastic bowl and put one in his mouth. "The Lakers are so bad they couldn't *buy* a win!"

Crossing his legs at the ankles, Max listened as Trey reminisced about taking Kiara to her first basketball game. Watching his brother amused him, made him think that true love did exist. He liked his bachelor lifestyle, but deep down he envied the fact that Trey and Derek had both found happiness—even though their relationships intervened with their "guys only" nights. They'd grown close in recent months, but these days his brothers spent most of their free time with their fiancées, and Max missed hanging out with them on a weekly basis. It bothered him that their poker nights, outings to Lou's Diner and workout sessions at Champions Boxing Gym would soon be a distant memory, but he reminded himself that he had a lot to be thankful for. He finally had a good re-

lationship with his brothers, his business was flourishing,
Taylor had made the honor roll, Reginald was showing
small signs of improvement—

And you kissed Jada! interjected his inner voice.

Max licked his lips. Tried to recall every single de-
tail of their spontaneous make-out session in the conference room. Grinned when he remembered how she'd
eagerly responded to his touch. How she'd wasted no
time stroking his chest with her soft, delicate hands. It
was more than just a kiss. Making out with her had been
the highlight of the party, a thrilling, mind-blowing moment Max wanted to experience again and again and
again. And he would. No doubt about it. But the next
time he kissed Jada he wouldn't hold back. Wouldn't
stop until he had his fill of her—if that was even possible. She was one hell of a kisser, and he wondered what
other skills she had. Did she enjoy taking the reins in
the bedroom? Was she a bold, sensuous lover?

Goose bumps rippled across his skin, then careened
down his spine. A light bulb went off in his head, burn-
ing brighter than a million stars. He'd spend the holidays with Jada, but keep it quiet. He didn't want anyone
to know they were lovers. Couldn't risk someone at the
agency finding out about their affair. He shuddered to
think what would happen if the truth was revealed. He
wasn't a sexual predator who propositioned his female
employees, and Max didn't want his business rivals to
soil his reputation. A Christmas fling was the perfect
antidote for his stress, and just thinking about hooking up with Jada in his office—bent over his desk, on
his leather chair, up against the bookshelf—made his
mouth wet.

Jada stuck her head inside the kitchen, beckoning
Max with her hands, and his thoughts scattered like

leaves in the autumn breeze. His eyes froze on her lips. He saw her mouth moving, but he didn't hear a word she said. Was blindsided by her beauty. Couldn't think straight, let alone speak. She'd ditched her hair bun for loose, silky curls, and her burgundy cut-out sweater, skinny jeans and suede booties made her look sexy as hell. If his brothers weren't in the kitchen, Max would have kissed her, but since he didn't want to embarrass Jada he remained in his seat. Clasped his hands in his lap so he couldn't reach out and stroke her dewy brown skin.

"Bro, snap out of it." Trey gave Max a shot in the arm. "Listen up. Jada's talking to you."

Blinking, he tore his gaze away from Jada's curves and straightened in his chair. Mad at himself for zoning out, he wore an apologetic smile. "I'm sorry. You were saying?"

"Taylor's finished getting ready for the dance. Come see. She looks incredible!"

She's not the only one. Max started to tell Jada he loved her hairstyle, but when he spotted Taylor standing in the middle of the staircase, his tongue froze inside his mouth. What in the world? Was this a sick joke?

His stomach churned and a lump formed in his throat, threatening to choke him dead. Max couldn't believe what he was seeing. Five hours ago, his daughter had left the house looking like an adorable tween, but she'd returned from the Third Street Promenade dressed in a provocative outfit. Taylor—his sweet, innocent daughter who used to love finger painting, *Dora the Explorer* and pony rides at Griffith Park—was wearing makeup, a pink strapless dress that revealed an immodest amount of skin and strappy, open-toe heels.

"Dad, what do you think?" Taylor asked, doing a twirl.

"I think you need to go upstairs and change."

The smile slid off her lips, and her face crumpled like a sheet of paper. "Y-y-you don't like my outfit," she stammered. "You don't think I'm beautiful?"

"Of course I do, honey, but your dress is inappropriate."

"No, it's not. Ms. Jada helped me pick it out, and she said it was perfect for a girl my age."

Every muscle in his body tensed. Max glanced at Jada, hoping she'd deny his daughter's claim, but to his surprise, she looked upset, not embarrassed, and glared at him as if *he* was the problem. He rarely got mad at Jada, but he was angry that she'd allowed his daughter to buy a dress that belonged in a pop star's closet, and struggled to control his temper. It was a challenge, but he spoke in a calm voice. "Go find something else to wear."

"But, Dad—"

"This isn't open for discussion. Put on something in your closet."

"I've worn everything in my closet a million times!" Poking out her bottom lip, Taylor folded her arms across her chest. "I bought this outfit specifically for the dance, and I love it."

"What I say goes, and you're not leaving the house in that dress."

"Max, I think she looks lovely—"

"No one asked you," he mumbled, casting a glance over his shoulder. Pretending not to notice the wounded expression on Jada's face, he said, "Stay out of this. It's none of your business."

Max respected Jada and was glad his daughter adored

her, too, but he didn't need any more unsolicited advice from her. When it came to parenting his daughter she was wrong. Taylor was a tween, not a college student, and he wasn't going to give her the freedom to do and wear whatever she wanted.

"I have to wear this dress," Taylor explained, her voice wobbling with emotion. "This is the kind of outfit all the girls will be wearing at the dance, and I want to fit in with my friends."

Max held his ground, wouldn't let his daughter have her way just because she was pouting. If he did, she'd never learn to respect him or anyone else, and he didn't want her to become a spoiled, disrespectful child. "You can change, or you can stay home. It's your decision."

"Come on!" she whined, stomping her foot on the ground. "I have nothing else to wear."

"Yes, you do, and this is not open for discussion, so do as you're told."

Tension consumed the air, polluting the space with hostility and anger. Frowning, Max glanced over his shoulder and peered into the kitchen. He could hear the TV blaring, Kevin Hart's shrill, animated voice and the whirl of the microwave. His brothers were watching a movie and talking smack, but their hearty chuckles didn't bolster his spirits.

"This is so unfair," Taylor complained. "And you're being mean."

"I want you to go to the dance and have a good time with your friends—"

"No, you don't. You're bossy and controlling, and you're trying to ruin my life!"

Her expression was grim, but Max was determined to stand his ground. He had to teach his daughter to make better choices. To be a leader, not a follower. He was her father, not her friend, and nothing mattered more to him than raising a confident young woman who respected herself and her body. The hyper-sexualization of females in society was frightening, and he'd seen first-hand the negative effect on teenage girls. For that reason, he paid close attention to everything his daughter did. Max wanted Taylor to be happy, but there was no way in hell he was letting her go to the dance in a dress that belonged in Rihanna's closet.

A thought struck him. What if Taylor refused to change? What if she decided to stay home? After the dance, she was supposed to have a sleepover at her best friend's house, but if she changed her mind he'd have to cancel his trip to Maui for Wendell Coleman's birthday bash. The three-time Tony Award winner had five teenage daughters, and Max knew his favorite client would understand what he was going through with Taylor. Wouldn't begrudge him for missing the star-studded event at his favorite resort, but to be on the safe side, he'd ask Jada to arrange to have the actor's birthday gift delivered to his LA mansion first thing tomorrow.

"I love this dress, and I'm wearing it to the dance. You can't stop me." Raising her bent shoulders, Taylor fervently nodded her head. "I'm calling Mom. She'll agree with me."

"It won't change anything. This is my house, my rules, and my word is law."

Max started to tell Taylor she was a beautiful girl who didn't need to wear makeup or revealing clothes to be noticed, but when tears filled her eyes and spilled down her cheeks, he broke off speaking. It hurt Max to see her cry. Filled with sympathy, he moved toward the staircase with his arms outstretched.

"Don't touch me!" Taylor spun around and marched

upstairs, her shiny black hair swishing across her bare back. "Leave me alone! I don't want to talk to you."

"Taylor, don't speak to me like that. I'm your father and you will respect me…"

Max wanted to climb the stairs, to follow Taylor into her bedroom, but a hand gripped his forearm, stopping him in his tracks.

"Max, calm down. You're shouting. You're scaring her."

"Don't tell me what to do. Taylor's my daughter, not yours, and I don't need your help."

Jada's head jerked back as if she'd been slapped across the face, and she released his arm.

"This is all my fault," he said. "I should have taken Taylor shopping myself, instead of letting her go out with you, but I thought you could handle it. I thought you'd respect my wishes."

Jada didn't speak, but her dark, menacing gaze chilled Max to the bone.

Chapter 12

Leave before it's too late, or you'll end up saying something you regret! Jada dismissed the thought, refused to heed the warning blaring in her mind. Her inner voice told her to grab her things and leave the mansion, but Jada wasn't going to run off just because Max had yelled at her. His words hurt, but she concealed her emotions. Wouldn't give him the satisfaction of seeing her cry. Stepping forward, Jada met his dark, hostile gaze. Didn't flinch when his jaw clenched and his face darkened. She'd never lost her temper before, let alone hit anyone, but the urge to punch Max was so overwhelming her hands curled into fists.

Jada straightened her bent shoulders. Ignored her damp palms and quivering limbs. She knew what she had to do. She had to take a stand. To speak the truth. Couldn't remain silent because Max was her boss and she was afraid of getting on his bad side. Screw that. And this time she wouldn't let him silence her. Nothing was going to stop her from setting him straight. From showing him the errors of his ways. He'd treated Taylor horribly, had been harsh and unreasonable, and he owed his daughter an apology. "Max, you overreacted about Taylor's outfit, and the things you said to her were incredibly hurtful."

Max scoffed, shook his head as if it was the most ludicrous thing he'd ever heard. "Are you kidding me? Taylor has no business wearing makeup, her hairstyle is too mature for a ten-year-old, and her dress is completely inappropriate."

"Why? Because it doesn't reach her ankles?"

"No, because I don't want horny, pubescent boys ogling my daughter. I'm her father, Jada. It's my job to protect her, and that's what I'm going to do, whether you like it or not."

"Protect her from what? She's going to a chaperoned school dance, not Coachella." Jada wanted to grip his shoulders and shake some sense into him, but she kept her hands at her sides. "The problem isn't Taylor's outfit, Max. It's you."

Max raised an eyebrow. He stood perfectly still, like a guard standing outside Buckingham Palace, but Jada could tell by his narrowed gaze and stiff posture that he was upset. Pissed that she'd disagreed with him. Determined to get through to him, she wore a sympathetic expression on her face and softened her tone of voice. "Taylor isn't five anymore. She's ten. A tween. A feisty, spunky girl who's interested in makeup and boys, and the sooner you come to terms with who she is, the better off you'll be. And Taylor, too."

"Thanks for your concern," he said with false cheerfulness, "but this is *my* family, *my* daughter, and I know what's best for her. Not you. Don't worry, Jada. I've got this."

Vibrating with anger, Jada pursed her lips together to trap the curse on her tongue inside her mouth. She couldn't believe his nerve, the smug, confident grin on his mouth. Who did Max think he was? The second coming of Christ? It took every ounce of self-control Jada had not to storm into the great room, snatch a pillow off the brown suede couch and beat him with it. *How dare Max speak to me like that!* she raged, seething inwardly. *I did nothing wrong!* He's *the one who insulted Taylor and made her cry! Not me!*

Jada took a deep, calming breath. Glanced outside the window and admired the clear, picture-perfect sky. Her gaze swept over the expansive grounds. It was beautifully landscaped, with vibrant floral gardens, shady trees and a lily pond. The sprawling six-acre estate in the most exclusive neighborhood in Los Angeles was fit for a king, and the muted earth tones throughout the main floor created a tranquil mood, but Jada felt stressed, not relaxed. In university, Max had had dreams of becoming an architect, and his keen eye for design had been beneficial when he purchased and renovated the Malibu mansion. Every room offered stunning views of the ocean, the open-floor concept was warm and inviting, and framed family portraits hung on the ivory walls.

This makes no sense, Jada thought, staring at a photograph of Max hugging Taylor. *Max loves his daughter more than anything else in the world, so why would he hurt her feelings? Why would he make her cry?*

"Before you go, let me make one thing clear..."

Curious about what Max was about to say, Jada tore her gaze away from the photograph and gave him her undivided attention. Stopped trying to figure out why Max had blown up at Taylor.

"You're my assistant, not my therapist or a family counselor," he continued in a stern voice. "In future, I'd appreciate if you didn't intervene when I'm disciplining my daughter."

Heat burned her cheeks and shame crawled across her skin. Jada wanted the ground to open up and swallow her. She couldn't think of anything worse than being scolded by Max, in *his* house, with his daughter and brothers listening in, and realized she'd overstayed her welcome. Crossed the line. This wasn't her family. Max was her boss—period—and now Jada knew no matter what she said or did that would never change. They'd kissed last night, and she'd fooled herself into believing it meant something to Max, that he cared about her, but he didn't. He didn't respect her or value her opinion, and Jada had to leave his estate before things got worse.

Max cleared his throat. "One more thing. Keep your thoughts and opinions about my parenting skills to yourself from now on, because I don't want to hear it. Understood? I won't let you or anyone else undermine me in front of Taylor."

Her hands were shaking, but she grabbed her purse off the mahogany table and forced a smile, one that concealed the anger simmering inside her. "Max, you know what? You're right," she said, nodding her head. "I'm a lowly administrative assistant. Who am I to tell you what to do? Or advise you about how to parent your daughter? I'm a nobody."

Max tried to interrupt her, to clarify what he'd said seconds earlier, but Jada cut him off.

"*You* asked for my help, but the moment I disagreed

with you, you decided my opinion was worthless, and now that I know how you *really* feel about me, I can't work for you."

"You're twisting my words. I never said that."

"You didn't have to. I'm quite skilled at reading between the lines…" Her voice wobbled, but she pushed past her emotions and spoke her mind. "I quit. I'll submit an official letter of resignation first thing Monday morning."

Fear flashed in his eyes. "Jada, you can't quit. I need you. You're the heart and soul of Millennium Talent Agency, and I'd be lost without you."

"Nonsense. You're the legendary Max Moore. One of the most revered talent agents in the city. You don't need me or anyone else. You've got this, remember?"

Her mind made up, she turned and strode through the foyer.

Max slid in front of her, blocking her path. His cologne washed over her, and for a moment, Jada forgot why she was mad at him. He licked his lips, and tingles flooded her body.

"You're quitting because I disagreed with you?" he asked, his eyebrows jammed together in a crooked line. "Because we argued about Taylor's outfit for her school dance?"

No, I'm quitting because I love you, and I'm tired of pretending I don't.

"Thanks for everything, Max. It was an honor to work for you. I've learned so much."

"I won't let you quit. We're a team, Jada, and I need you at the agency."

Scared her emotions would get the best of her and she'd burst into tears if she spoke, Jada stepped past Max and yanked open the front door. He called out to her, but she didn't stop. Ignored his apologies. Increased her pace. Fleeing the multimillion-dollar estate with the feng shui fountain, the vibrant flower garden and the winding cobblestone driveway, she willed her heart not to fail and her legs not to buckle.

Jada deactivated the alarm, slipped inside her car and started it. Anxious to leave, she put on her seat belt, then sped through the wrought-iron gates. In her rearview mirror, she spotted Max and his brothers standing on the driveway and wondered if they were discussing her dramatic exit. Jada dismissed the thought, told herself it didn't matter what the Moore brothers were doing. Max was her past, not her future, and she had to stop thinking about him. Gripping the steering wheel, Jada swallowed hard, blinking away the tears in her eyes.

An hour later, Jada parked in front of her condo, turned off the ignition and dropped her face in her hands. Christmas music played from inside her purse, and she knew from the ringtone that it was her cousin calling, but Jada didn't feel like talking to Aubree. Not now. Feared if she did she'd choke up. And even though she wanted to vent about what happened with Max, she didn't want her cousin to worry about her. Or race over to her apartment with a bucket of cookie dough ice cream and an armload of chick flicks.

Jada stepped out of the car. Retrieving her shopping bags from the trunk, she spotted children in red velvet Santa hats playing soccer at the park across the street and joggers, dripping in sweat, racing up the block. She'd lived in the neighborhood for a year, and had easily made friends in the close-knit community. It was a safe area, her neighbors were young and worldly, and best of all, it was a short twenty-minute drive to her father's apartment.

Jada dragged herself inside her condo, dumped her bags on the hardwood floor and dropped into her favorite armchair. Her two-bedroom Santa Monica townhome was smaller than Max's kitchen, but Jada loved everything about her condo. It was bright and cozy, filled with natural sunlight, and decorated with vintage posters, colorful area rugs and suede furniture. Yesterday, while watching *This Christmas* on TV, she'd put up her pine tree and decorated the living room with ribbons, tree lights and greenery, but the soothing, refreshing scent in the air didn't alleviate her stress. Didn't stop her from reliving her argument with Max in her mind.

What a day, she thought, exhaling a deep breath. She'd gone shopping with Taylor, then argued with Max. She hadn't planned on resigning, but in the heat of the moment it had seemed like the right thing to do. The only thing to do. Though now she regretted her rash decision. Jada had enough money saved to pay her bills for three months, but she'd go stir-crazy being home every day, with nowhere to go and nothing to do. First thing Monday morning, she was going to the unemployment office. Working part-time was better than sitting around in her condo thinking about Max, and Jada was hopeful she'd have another administrative position in the New Year, because returning to Millennium Talent Agency wasn't an option.

Jada blinked back tears, staring up at the ceiling until the moment passed and her vision cleared. Her instincts had been wrong. Max wasn't the right man for her. Like her ex, he didn't respect her, and that was reason enough to stay away from him—

Taylor, too, added her inner voice. *You have to make a clean break.*

Sadness filled her heart. Jada adored the tween, but she'd never get over Max if she was still communicating with his daughter, and although she knew Taylor would be upset, she made a mental note to cancel their Sunday afternoon plans at the holiday ice rink.

Her gaze strayed to the coffee table and landed on the framed photograph of her family, and for some strange reason Jada wondered what her dad and siblings would think of Max. Would her father approve of him? Would he get along well with her family? Would they like him? Of course they would, she thought, dismissing every doubt. Everyone always did. Max was more than just a handsome face. He was personable, had a fun-loving nature and an eclectic taste in music, food and movies. Over the years, she'd seen him work his magic on difficult people, so making a connection with her loud, lovable family would be a breeze. *Not that it matters*, she told herself, blinking back tears. *Max doesn't respect me, and we'll never be a couple.*

Her cell phone buzzed, and Jada fished it out of her purse. Her eyes widened. It was six o'clock! She'd been sitting in the living room for over an hour, staring aimlessly at the ivory walls, thinking about Max. Try as she might, she couldn't shake her melancholy mood, couldn't stop wondering how Taylor was doing, and if she'd gone to her school dance as planned.

Jada punched in her password, read her newest text message and surged to her feet, knocking her purse off her lap. Shoot! Shazir was on his way to her apartment to pick her up for the Prescott George party. The event was for members, their family and guests, but Jada didn't want to be anywhere near Max. Not because she hated him, but because she was scared her emotions would get the best of her and she'd lose her temper again. Busy with Taylor, she'd forgotten to respond to Shazir's earlier text message, and now he thought she was his date for the party. It wasn't going to happen. No way, no how.

Hoping to catch Shazir before he left his house, Jada dialed his cell number and put her iPhone to her ear. He answered on the first ring, and relief flowed through her body. His confidence was evident in his flirtatious greeting, but Jada wasn't moved by his performance. Guys like Shazir were a dime a dozen in LA, and although Jada enjoyed his company, she knew they'd never be more than friends.

"Hello, Beautiful. I know you're anxious to see me, but I'll be there soon," Shazir said, his tone dripping with pride. "I hope you're dressed and ready to go to the Prescott George holiday mixer because I'll be at your condo in ten minutes."

"I'm sorry, but I can't go. I meant to call you earlier, but it's been a crazy-busy day."

"Of course you're going. You're my date."

No, I'm not! Jeez, what's wrong with these LA men? Don't they listen?

"Reginald is showing signs of improvement, and the Moore boys want to celebrate the good news with their friends and family at the Prescott George headquarters," he added. "You have to come. It's a momentous occasion, and I'd hate for you to miss it."

Jada was glad Reginald was feeling better, and hoped his health continued to improve, but in light of everything that had happened that afternoon with Max, she didn't think it was a good idea to attend the party. He wouldn't want her there, and that was reason enough to stay home.

"Furthermore, I have a very important business proposition to discuss with you," Shazir continued. "One I know you'll be excited about. Trust me. It's big. Huge. Life-changing."

Intrigued, Jada stared down at her cell phone. She wondered what Shazir had up his sleeve and asked him point-blank. "I'm listening. Tell me more."

"Not now. We'll talk later, after the party."

"Shazir, I'm not going. I don't belong at the Prescott George holiday mixer."

"Is that what Max told you?" He scoffed. "Don't listen to him. Forget him. It doesn't matter what he thinks."

How can I forget a man I've been crushing on for years? A man whose smile makes my heart flutter and my knees weak? Jada hesitated, took a moment to think things through. Going to the party with Shazir was a bad idea, but he wouldn't take no for an answer. Insisted she attend the event as his special guest, and promised to be a perfect gentleman.

"You're going, and that's final."

Jada opened her mouth to protest, but the dial tone buzzed in her ear. She redialed Shazir's cell number, but his voice mail came on. She texted him, but no response. Left with no other options, she marched into her bedroom to get ready for the Prescott George party.

Butterflies flooded her stomach. She wasn't pumped about schmoozing with multimillionaires and powerful business executives; she was excited about seeing Max again, and secretly hoped he'd apologize and beg her not to quit Millennium Talent Agency.

An apology? Keep dreaming! quipped her inner voice in a shrill, sarcastic tone. *You have a better chance of being struck by lightning during a snowstorm!*

Chapter 13

The Prescott George headquarters were located on the twelfth floor of the Fine Arts Building, a historic cultural monument in downtown Los Angeles. As Shazir led Jada through the grand, sophisticated space, bragging about his many contributions to Prescott George, Jada admired the palatial ambience.

Jada composed herself and closed her gaping mouth as they entered the great room. Filled with gleaming marble floors, decorative chandeliers, and eye-catching artwork and sculptures, the penthouse reminded her of a museum. There were large sitting areas surrounded by smaller, enclosed offices for board members, meeting spaces and two grand ballrooms for social events. The penthouse and the elegantly dressed guests milling about exuded wealth and opulence, and Jada felt out of place, as if she didn't belong. And she didn't. From the moment Shazir had picked her up and ushered her inside his yellow convertible, Jada had doubts about attending the holiday mixer. Shazir must have sensed her unease, because he moved in close and tightened his hold around her waist. Pressed his body against hers. The only thing Shazir loved more than boasting about his fabulous jet-setting life was posting about it on social media, and when he suggested they take a selfie, she politely declined. She didn't want Shazir to think she was interested in him romantically. She wasn't. Her heart yearned for Max, her body, too, and she didn't want anyone else. And if not for her curiosity about Shazir's lucrative business proposition, she never would have agreed to be his date for the holiday mixer.

Her thoughts returned to minutes earlier. In the car, while driving to the party, Shazir had flirted with her nonstop and complimented her outfit so many times Jada lost count. She'd paired her green wrap dress with gold tassel earrings, bangles and a beaded clutch purse. Her metallic ankle-strap pumps gave the outfit a youthful edge, and every time Jada glanced in the passenger-side mirror a smile overwhelmed her mouth. She loved her new look and had never felt sexier. Though she'd wished Shazir would quit ogling her. When he stopped at an intersection, he'd tried to kiss her, but she'd turned her face, causing his lips to graze her cheek. Annoyed, she'd glared at him. Was that why he'd asked her to be his date? Because he wanted to put the moves on her? Because he thought he could lure her into his bed? Put off by his sexual advances, Jada reminded Shazir they were friends and nothing more, and told him if he crossed the line again she was going home. Mumbling an apology, he'd jacked up the volume on the stereo and kept his eyes on the road and off her cleavage for the rest of the drive.

The great room held a strong, piquant scent, and her mouth watered at the delicious aromas wafting in the air. Tuxedo-clad servers holding silver trays offered candy cane martinis and star-shaped salmon capers to guests. The instrumental version of "Winter Wonderland" wafted through the grand room, and decorative glass vases filled with poinsettias beautified the round tables. The towering Christmas tree in the corner of the room twinkled with lights and silver ornaments, and lush green wreaths hung on the walls.

Jada stopped abruptly, couldn't get her legs to move. She spotted Max standing in front of the fireplace and sucked in a breath. While Shazir bragged about his prized motorcycle collection and his palatial homes around the world, Jada tried to get her body under control. She had to stop shaking, sweating and fidgeting. No doubt, Max would be surprised to see her at the party with Shazir, but she had to remain calm, no matter what. Couldn't wear her heart on her sleeve, or do something stupid like crash through the emergency exit to escape.

Her gaze slid down his shoulders and lingered on his chest. *Mercy*, she thought, unable to control her wayward thoughts. *He looks good enough to eat, and I'm starving!* He was dressed in his trademark Armani suit, a burgundy tie and polished leather shoes, and it was impossible not to stare at him. To envision him naked in her bed. To desire another kiss. She couldn't take her eyes off him, tried but failed miserably. Jada willed him to turn around, to notice her across the room, but he was standing beside Reginald's wheelchair, chatting with several distinguished-looking men, oblivious to the world around him.

"I'm glad you agreed to be my date tonight," Shazir

said. "You look sensational on my arm, and we make a formidable couple, like a younger, sexier version of the Obamas…"

Jada forced herself not to roll her eyes. *If you say so, but I'm not interested.*

"Damn, you're so fine I'd follow you off a bridge if you jumped!"

His hearty chuckle made her laugh. "You're crazy."

"And you're hardworking, intelligent and sincere. That's why I want you to come work for me." Shazir lowered his mouth to her ear and spoke in a husky voice. "You're the total package, and I need someone with your skill and expertise to be my right hand."

"Shazir, I already have a full-time job."

Guilt pricked her conscience, but Jada ignored it, pretended not to notice the heaviness in her chest. She didn't feel comfortable telling Shazir about her argument with Max. The less he knew about her problems, the better. Jada didn't want to tell him she'd quit her job, feared if she did he'd rub it in Max's face, and she didn't want her ex-boss to be mad at her.

A waiter approached, but Shazir dismissed him with a flick of his hand and continued his pitch. "My assistant quit two weeks ago, and everyone the temp agency sent over was a complete disaster," he complained. "They were lazy and incompetent, and I fired all of them. Needless to say, I'm desperate to find a suitable replacement, and I have my sights set on you."

Realization dawned as Jada slowly nodded her head. Now everything made sense. She finally understood why Shazir had asked her out, why he was relentlessly pursuing her. He needed a new assistant and thought he could lure her away from Millennium Talent Agency, but it wasn't going to happen. Max would lose it if she went to work for his business rival, and although they weren't friends anymore, Jada would never do anything to purposely hurt him. "Shazir, thanks for thinking of me, but I can't work for you—"

"How much is Max paying you? I'll double your salary and give you a hefty signing bonus. Be smart, Jada. Five grand can buy a *lot* of Christmas gifts."

Dollar signs flashed in her mind, and her mouth fell open. She'd been toying with the idea of returning to school next year to finish her degree in human resources, and if she accepted Shazir's job offer she could use the money from the signing bonus to pay her tuition. Every year, Max gave his employees a bottle of expensive wine and a Christmas bonus, but since she'd resigned that afternoon she probably wouldn't be entitled to the gift.

Jada told herself it didn't matter, not to sweat it. Money wasn't everything, and she'd rather be unemployed than work for someone who didn't respect her. "Why me?" she asked. "Why do you want to hire me to be your personal assistant? What makes me so special?"

"Max is always bragging about you being his secret weapon, says you're the heart and soul of Millennium Talent Agency, and I could use someone like you in my corner. So, when my assistant quit I figured this was the perfect opportunity to steal you away from the competition. Was I right?"

Jada didn't answer, dodged his gaze. She needed a moment to collect her thoughts. Jada was no fool; she knew what Shazir wanted, what his motives were. He wanted to make Max jealous and uncover his secrets, but Jada would never betray her former boss. It was a tempting offer, and she could definitely use the money, but she couldn't work for Shazir. And not just because he hated Max. She didn't trust him, and couldn't imagine being his assistant, not even for double her salary.

"There's no rush," he said casually, squeezing her shoulders. "The agency's closed for the holidays, and I leave for Aspen tomorrow, so I don't need your answer right now. Take a few days to think about it, and let me know what you decide in the New Year."

There was nothing to think about, but Jada nodded her head, as if she was going to consider his offer. A server appeared with drinks. Shazir grabbed two champagne flutes from off his tray and shoved one into Jada's hand. "This Christmas," came on the stereo system, and hearing the soulful, upbeat song brightened her mood. Humming the lyrics, she swayed her body to the music. Why was she stressing about seeing Max? Worried about how he would react when he found out she was Shazir's date? It didn't matter what Max thought, didn't matter that they were at odds. It was Christmas, her favorite time of year, and she was going to have fun at the party.

"Jada, I'll be right back." Shazir straightened his navy blue tie. "I need to touch base with Christina North and the board chairman about the Rent-a-Bachelor charity fund-raiser. I've raised more money than anyone else in the organization, and I deserve to be publicly recognized. If not for me, the fund-raiser would have tanked!"

As Shazir left, a female waiter appeared with appetizers. Taking a napkin, Jada helped herself to some hors d'oeuvre and made small talk with the silver-haired gentleman standing nearby. Out of the corner of her eye, she spotted Alexis across the room, giggling and cuddling with Derek. The mom-to-be waved, and Jada did, too. A sucker for a fairy-tale romance, she watched the love-struck couple for several seconds. She liked the

former supermodel, and was happy that Alexis had reunited with her high school sweetheart and was expect-
ing her first child. Unlike other brides, Alexis wasn't
excited about dress fittings, cake tastings and bridal
shows; she was thrilled about marrying her soul mate,
and Jada hoped the model had the wedding of their
dreams and a healthy baby.

Jada touched her stomach, couldn't help wondering
what it was like to be pregnant. From the moment she'd
met Max, she'd dreamed of marrying him and having
his babies, and even though she knew they'd never be
a couple, Jada still fantasized about being a wife and
mother. Over the last two years, she'd met plenty of
great guys, but she'd ignored them because she was
holding out hope for Max. That had been a mistake.
Just because none of them gave her butterflies didn't
mean she shouldn't consider them. Why not give them
a chance? It couldn't hurt. And dating someone new
was a hell of a lot better than sitting around, pining for
Max during the holiday season. Max wasn't interested
in her, and she had to accept it. She had to move on with
her life, and she would.

Clearing her mind, Jada rejoined the conversation,
chatting and laughing with everyone in the group. Several of Max's business associates, whom she'd met nu-
merous times, didn't recognize her because of her new
look, and their effusive praise made heat flood her
cheeks. Jada hated being the center of attention, and
the more they gushed about her appearance, the more
embarrassed she was.

"You're a great conversationalist, and I'd love to take
you out sometime." The cardiologist in the checkered
bow tie and navy suit asked for her cell number. "If

you're free tomorrow, we could have dinner at Nobu. How does that sound?"

Lust shone in his eyes, and his broad grin showcased each one of his pearly white teeth. Jada wasn't attracted to the short, stocky bachelor, but she considered his request. Her cousins had canceled their plans for Sunday, and Jada had nothing else to do, so why not have dinner with the successful cardiologist from Bel-Air? If nothing else, they'd have a nice meal at the chic five-star restaurant, and maybe even spot a celebrity or two.

Warming to the idea, Jada returned his smile. Bound and determined to forget Max, she opened her purse and took out a business card. But when the cardiologist plucked it out of her hand and promised to call her later, Jada felt worse, not better, and knew she'd made a mistake. Once again, her gaze found Max. He was at the bar, surrounded by a bevy of beauties, no doubt wooing them with his charm. Max was it for her, the only man she wanted, and that sucked. *How am I supposed to move on with my life when I can't stop obsessing about Max?*

Max faked a smile, nodded as if he was listening to the redhead's long, convoluted story about her audition with Tyler Perry weeks earlier, but he was actually watching Jada on the sly. He still couldn't believe she'd arrived at the party with Shazir, a man he despised, and wondered for the umpteenth time if she'd lied to him about them being lovers. *God, I hope not*, he thought, downing the rest of the vodka tonic.

"If you were my man, I'd already be a household name, and have my picks of jobs."

"Me, too," chirped a former child star. "Let's hook up later. You won't regret it."

The other women at the bar spoke at once, shouting to be heard, but Max ignored them. His friends and family didn't believe him, but it was hard finding love in the gold-digger capital of the world. Every woman he met in LA had ulterior motives. They were more interested in what he could do for them than in getting to know him as a person. And forget meeting Taylor. They knew nothing about kids, didn't want to learn, and complained when he skipped social events to spend quality time with his daughter. He wasn't ready to settle down, but if he did find love again it wouldn't be with someone in the entertainment business. It would be with someone humble, loving and sincere, who enjoyed the simple pleasures in life like breakfast in bed, picnics in the park, long drives through the countryside and afternoons spent binge-watching his favorite TV shows on Netflix.

"Max, are you going to the Golden Globe Awards next month? I'd *love* to be your date."

"Get in line," joked a news reporter. "We all want to be his plus-one to the awards show."

Tuning the conversation out, he focused his attention on his stunning administrative assistant. Max checked her out from head to toe. He liked how her makeup enhanced her natural beauty, how her money-green dress skimmed her curves and how her high heels elongated her brown, silky legs.

Damn, she's been hiding all that body under shapeless clothes all this time? Why? he wondered. *It doesn't make sense. Most women play up their looks, not downplay them, and females with remarkable beauty like Jada often use their looks to get ahead.*

Max raised his shoulders, straightened to his full height. He'd never expected to see Jada at the Prescott

George party, and watching her socialize with other organization members pissed him off. After she'd quit and stormed out of his house, his brothers had joined him in the foyer, wearing grim expressions on their faces. They'd threatened to disown him if he didn't apologize to Taylor, and encouraged him to make amends with Jada, too.

"You guys agree with Jada?" he'd asked, unable to believe what he was hearing from his siblings. "But you're *my* brothers. You're supposed to have my back."

"We do, but we're not going to tell you you're right when you're wrong, and, bro, you're a hundred percent wrong on this one." Trey had vigorously nodded his head. "You were mean to Taylor and you should go upstairs and apologize."

"And you were horrible to Jada, too," Derek had added. "You're so afraid of striking out at love and getting hurt again you can't even see that Jada's in love with you."

Flabbergasted, Max had lost his voice, couldn't speak. What? Jada? But she was his right hand, not a potential love interest. Nothing made sense to him, and he couldn't understand why his brothers were encouraging him to pursue his longtime assistant.

"Open your eyes, bro, before it's too late," Trey had warned. "Women like Jada are hard to find, and if you take too long to make your move someone else will swoop in and steal her right from under your nose. Someone suave and charismatic like your archrival."

"Shazir might be a lot of things, but he's no fool," Derek had said in a no-nonsense tone of voice. "He knows a good woman when he sees one, and he'll do everything in his power to get Jada in bed. Is that what you want? To see her on the arm of another man?"

The word *No* had blared in his mind, but he'd kept his thoughts to himself.

Scared his brothers would make good on their threat and beat him up, he'd gone upstairs to make things right with Taylor. It hadn't been easy, but he'd swallowed his pride and apologized to her for losing his temper. He'd wiped the tears from her eyes, told her how much he loved her and promised to stop treating her like a kid. To smooth things over, he'd agreed to let Taylor wear the pink strapless dress—with a cardigan—and she'd given him a big hug. Back downstairs, she'd posed for dozens of pictures with her doting uncles, and by the time Taylor had left for the dance with her best friend, she was smiling, giggling and blowing kisses.

Max had hoped his brothers would leave when Taylor did, but they'd followed him into his master suite, giving him unsolicited advice about Jada. They'd advised him to send her flowers, then call and ask her out, but he'd refused. He'd reminded them that he was her boss and he didn't believe in mixing business with pleasure. A Christmas fling was one thing; a long-term relationship was another. Though Max didn't know what Jada wanted. Was she the relationship type? Was she eager to be a wife and mother, or content playing the field? Would she be interested in a fling, no strings attached? Max had dismissed his thoughts and his brothers' suggestions. "It won't work. I'm her boss. It wouldn't look good."

Derek had cocked an eyebrow. "Jada resigned, remember?"

"That's right," Trey had said, with a broad grin. "She doesn't work for you anymore, so you're not breaking the rules. And if I were you, I'd call her ASAP."

Max blinked, gave his head a shake to clear his mind.

His heart brightened and hope surged through his veins. Jada was alone! She was standing beside the Christmas tree, snapping pictures, and Max knew if he didn't make his move now he might not get another chance. All night, he'd watched other men approach her, and wanted a moment alone with her, too, without Shazir or anyone else interrupting them.

Intent on reaching her, Max stalked across the room with one thought on his mind. He grabbed a candy cane martini off a waiter's tray and joined her in front of the ridiculously tall Christmas tree in the corner of the room. Her perfume filled his nostrils, and the floral, fruity scent instantly calmed him. Max couldn't recall ever being this tense, not even when he'd met his idol, Sidney Poitier, at the Palm Springs International Film Festival last year, and hoped he wouldn't embarrass himself. Although he knew she'd never laugh at him. Jada just wasn't that girl. She didn't have a mean bone in her body and treated everyone with kindness. But when Jada glanced in his direction, and the smile slid off her lips, his confidence deserted him and sweat drenched his palms.

"A drink for the most beautiful woman in the room," he said with a nod and a grin.

Jada stared at the glass, then back at him, and shook her head. "No, thanks. I'm good."

"Looks like you lost your date to an Instagram model."

Following the route of his gaze, she shrugged as if she didn't care who Shazir was getting cozy with. "It's to be expected. Shazir is a big-shot Hollywood executive, and I'm an average-looking girl from Inglewood—"

Stunned by her admission, he interrupted her mid-sentence. "That's the most ludicrous thing I've ever heard. You're smart, witty and beautiful, and there's nothing average about you."

Her eyes narrowed, but Max didn't understand why. Clearing his throat, he put the cocktail glass down on a nearby table and wore a sincere expression on his face. In full swing now, the party was filled with the most successful and influential people in LA, but Max only had eyes for Jada. "You don't believe me?"

"Of course not. Men don't want smart girls with nice personalities. They want girls with big boobs and huge asses, girls who'll put out on the first date."

"Not me. I prefer females with class and substance. Like you." Winking good-naturedly, Max stepped forward and cupped her chin in his hand. Her skin was soft and warm against his. Everyone at the party could see them, but he didn't care. Nothing mattered more to him than making things right with Jada, and he would. "You're intelligent and perceptive and I think the world of you."

Jada laughed, and the loud, shrill sound pierced his eardrum. A scowl darkened her face and bruised her lips. The urge to kiss her was overwhelming, more powerful than gale force winds, but he ignored the needs of his flesh and stuffed his hands into the pockets of his dress pants. It wasn't the time or the place to make a move on her. Not when she was giving him attitude. Max knew he deserved the cold shoulder, but still... He wasn't used to Jada being mad at him, and he didn't like it. Wanted them to go back to being cool with each other, and hoped he'd be able to prove to her that he was being sincere.

"I don't believe you."

Out of the corner of his eye, he spotted Shazir getting cozy with the full-figured model, and thanked his lucky stars. He hoped the talent agent spent the rest of the night with the woman and far away from Jada. "Why would I lie? You're important to me, and I care about you."

"If that was true, you wouldn't have insulted me this afternoon when I tried to talk to you about Taylor. You would have listened to me with an open heart, instead of dismissing my opinion." Jada tucked her purse under her arm. "Now, if you'll excuse me, I need to use the ladies' room. Enjoy the rest of your evening."

Max watched Jada exit the great room, sashay down the hallway and out of sight. He couldn't recall ever feeling so low. *Damn*, he thought, rubbing a hand along the back of his neck. *Walking on water wouldn't be this hard!* He had to make things right with Jada. Tonight, before the chasm between them grew, and he lost her forever. He'd screwed up, and if he wanted her back in his life he had to go all out. Up his game.

An idea came to him, and his frown morphed into a smile. He'd never chased down a woman before, had never begged anyone for forgiveness, but that was exactly what he was going to do. He was willing to be vulnerable if it meant seeing Jada smile again. His pulse sped up as memories of their first kiss came to mind. Just the thought of kissing her, of feeling her warm, soft body pressed hard against his, made his mouth dry.

Glancing around the room to ensure the coast was clear, Max marched purposely through the doors and down the corridor with one thought on his mind: seducing Jada. And Max knew just what to do to make his fantasies about his assistant come true.

Chapter 14

Jada studied her reflection in the oval-shaped mirror in the ladies' washroom and liked what she saw. She still couldn't believe how different she looked with curly hair, professional makeup and a designer dress, and she hoped she'd be able to maintain her chic new appearance in the New Year. She washed her hands with soap, dried them with a paper towel and dumped it in the trash can.

The door swung open, and several females drowning in diamonds and heavy makeup sashayed inside, giggling uncontrollably. Jada recognized them from the party, recalled seeing the quartet huddled up with Max at the bar and wondered which woman was his date. The Gabrielle Union look-alike? The female in the black mesh cocktail dress? Or the Caribbean beauty with the mile-long legs and endearing accent?

Her shoulders drooped, caving under the weight

of her sadness. Did it matter who his date was? Who he was going home with tonight? Max was out of her league, a man who could have anyone he wanted, and it didn't matter how much she desired him—he'd never be her boyfriend.

Giving her head a shake to clear her thoughts, Jada straightened her gold chain-link necklace and fixed her tousled hair. Max had messed it up when he'd touched her. Damn him. He'd waltzed up to her, smelling dreamy and sounding smooth. Jada could listen to Max talk all day, and was so captivated by the sound of his voice she'd almost forgotten that she was mad at him. She'd wanted to ask him about Taylor, was curious to know if the tween had gone to her first school dance, but she was so anxious to get away from Max it had slipped her mind.

Her cell phone chimed and Jada retrieved it from her clutch purse. She'd received a group text from Delilah and Aubree, and reading the message from her cousins made her smile. Their busy schedules had prevented them from getting together last weekend for dinner, and Jada missed them. They wanted to go Christmas shopping at The Grove on Monday, and she agreed to meet her cousins at the mall at five o'clock.

Texting Aubree, she yanked open the bathroom door and strode down the dimly lit corridor. Her feet were on fire, begging to be soaked in warm water. Jada decided she was taking a bath the moment she got home. Yawning, she struggled to keep her eyes open. It had been a long, taxing day, and all she could think about was going home to unwind.

She checked her watch, saw that it was ten o'clock and wondered if her date was ready to go. Wishing she'd driven herself to the Fine Arts Building, she decided to call a cab to pick her up. Shazir was the life-of-the-party type, and loved to mingle and socialize for hours on end, and Jada didn't want to wait for him; she wanted to leave now. Not because she had something important to do at home, but because talking to Max had unnerved her and she feared if he touched her again she'd do something she'd regret—like kiss him.

Jada was so busy texting back and forth with her cousins she didn't see Max until she bumped into him. He folded his arms around her, and she melted against his chest. Jada liked being near him. His cologne enveloped her, making her feel warm and cozy, but when she remembered the hurtful things he'd said to her that afternoon she tried to break free of his hold. "What are you doing? I need to return to the party."

"A female guest booked Shazir for the rest of the night through the Rent-a-Bachelor fund-raiser, and they left a few minutes ago," he explained, gesturing to the elevator with a nod of his head. "Shazir couldn't find you, and asked me to tell you."

Of course he did! Jada thought, annoyed that he'd ditched her for someone else while she was in the ladies' room. *He's a modern-day Casanova who'll bed anything that moves!*

"Jada, don't sweat it. I'll take you home whenever you're ready."

"Don't worry about me. I can find my way home. Now please let go of me."

He tightened his hold around her waist. "Not until we talk."

"We already did, and to be honest, I'm all talked out. I have nothing else to say to you."

"Well, I have a lot to say, and I'm not leaving until I do."

Max didn't raise his voice, but Jada could tell by the

terse expression on his face that he was frustrated. Annoyed with her. Jada forced herself not to suck her teeth and roll her eyes. Didn't want to get on his bad side again. The last time she did, he'd let her have it, and hours later his insults still stung.

"I'm mad at myself for hurting your feelings, and I want to apologize for the way I acted this afternoon. I lost it when I saw Taylor all dressed up, and I know it probably doesn't make sense to you, but my heart broke when I realized she wasn't my little girl anymore..."

Moved by his confession and the vulnerability in his voice, Jada wiped the scowl off her face. In his eyes, Taylor was growing up too fast, and it was obvious Max was struggling to cope with the changes in his daughter. Jada sympathized with him and knew he was going through a rough patch with Taylor, but that was no excuse for his behavior.

As if reading her thoughts, he said, "I was an ass, but I hope you can find it in your heart to forgive me. I'm sorry I yelled at you, but it won't happen again."

"It better not, or I'll put my kickboxing training to good use and take you down!"

A grin curled his mouth. "Bring it on."

His gaze dropped from her eyes to her lips, sending shivers along her spine, but Jada stopped staring at his mouth and asked, "What happened with Taylor? Did she end up going to the dance, or is she home with the babysitter?"

"After you left, my brothers came down on me pretty hard for making Taylor cry, and threatened to kick my ass if I didn't make amends," he explained. "Needless to say, I apologized for upsetting her, and Taylor left for the party with her best friend as planned."

"I'm proud of you, Max. You did the right thing."

Lowering his mouth to her ear, he brushed his lips against her skin and spoke in a deep, throaty voice. "Damn, you feel good. Jada, I'm weak for you, and I'm not afraid to admit it. I've tried, but I can't stop thinking about that kiss in the conference room."

Jada held her breath, waiting, hoping, willing him to make the first move, but he didn't.

Something came over her, and she did something she'd never dreamed possible: she backed Max into the wall, gripped his suit jacket in her hands and kissed him. As if she was starving and he was dinner. Now that she'd resigned, she didn't have to worry about being on her best behavior or doing the right thing, and gave herself permission to lose control. To do what felt natural. What she wanted, what her flesh desired.

Jada was breathless, but she licked his lips, hungrily feasted on them. He tasted even better than she remembered. Caught up in the moment, she moaned and groaned inside his mouth. Couldn't stop. Massaging his chest through his dress shirt, she enjoyed feeling his hard muscles beneath her fingertips, and his erection against her thigh. Her inner voice told her to break off the kiss and flee the corridor, but her body had a mind of its own. And it wanted Max. Feeling confident, Jada whispered against his mouth. "Max, I want to make love to you… It's all I can think about…all I want… Come back to my place…"

Staring down at her, his expression filled with skepticism, he raised an eyebrow. "Jada, are you sure? You've had several cocktails tonight, and I think that might be the alcohol talking."

"I'm positive. I've wanted this for a long time, but I was scared to make the first move."

"Why? Because of Taylor?"

"No, because of you. You date centerfolds, and I'm just a simple girl from Inglewood—"

"You're stunning, and any man would be honored to have you on his arm."

Hope surged through her heart. More excited than a bride on her wedding day, Jada tried to wipe the smile off her face, but couldn't. "Including you?"

"Hell, yeah." Max nuzzled his chin against her bare shoulder. "And if I wasn't your boss I'd take you with me to Maui for the weekend."

"You're not my boss anymore. I resigned this afternoon."

"You can't quit. You're the best employee I have!"

"You'll survive. You always do. You're Max Don't-Need-Anyone Moore. You can do my job and yours, and make it look easy."

"Jada, you're wrong. I need you," he whispered against her ear. "More than you know."

His tone had a hint of sexual innuendo to it, and Jada liked it, loved how he wasn't afraid to speak his mind or kiss her publicly, out in the open, where anyone could see them.

"Come with me to Maui. I don't have a date for the party, and I want to be with you."

Closing her gaping mouth, Jada met his gaze. Convinced she'd misheard him, she said, "You want me to be your plus-one for Wendell Coleman's birthday bash?"

"Abso-freakin'-lutely. With those eyes and that smile, you'll easily wow the other guests."

His words floored her, but she hid her surprise. Acted like his compliment was no big deal, even though it made her heart smile. Traveling with Max to Maui was out of the question, but Jada had to admit she was tempted. She liked the idea of being alone with him in one of the most romantic cities in the world. In her mind, she imagined them frolicking on the beach, feeding each other tropical fruit, kissing under the stars and dancing in the light of the moon. Slamming the brakes on her fantasy before it took an erotic turn, Jada moved out of his arms. She feared that if she didn't she'd lose control again. "Does your invitation have anything to do with me arriving at the party with Shazir?"

Max grinned. "It's not *who* you arrive with that's important. It's who you *leave* with."

Touché, she conceded, hiding a smirk. *And I'd love to leave with you!*

"Shazir isn't the right man for you, but that's not what this is about." Max took her hand in his and squeezed it. "Kissing you last night stirred something inside me, and now I'm seeing you in a whole new light. I think we owe it to ourselves to explore these new feelings, and why not do it in beautiful, sunny Maui?"

Why not indeed? His gaze held her hostage. Her tongue was glued to the roof of her mouth, and it felt like her shoes were stuck to the hardwood floor, but Jada maintained her composure. Didn't break out in song and dance around the corridor, kicking up her heels.

"Jada, you're coming, and that's final," he announced. "I won't take no for an answer."

His lips covered her mouth, and her thoughts scattered. Max slid a hand under her dress, stroking her bottom, palming and squeezing it. No one had ever made her feel so desirable, and making out with Max in the darkened hallway gave Jada a rush. Made her want to continue their intimate party for two on his private jet.

Voices filled the corridor, startling her, and Jada

broke off the kiss before they gave the other guests an eyeful. Fanning her face with one hand, she straightened her dress with the other. *Where are my shoes? And why am I panting like a dog in heat?* Bracing her hand against the wall, she stuffed her feet back inside her stilettos, then fixed her hair. Jada couldn't wrap her mind around what had happened. She'd kissed Max? Licked his lips and massaged his chest? Groaned, moaned and begged him to make love to her?

"We should go. My jet is waiting at the Van Nuys Airport, ready for takeoff."

"But I have nothing to wear," she argued. "Hell, I don't even have a toothbrush."

"Don't sweat it. We'll swing by your apartment and get everything you need."

Her head spinning, Jada could only nod. *Is this actually happening or am I dreaming?*

Taking the hand he offered, she snuggled against his shoulder. Excitement rippled across her skin. He'd seduced her, one kiss at a time, and just the thought of making love to him made her panties wet. Jada wasn't going to worry about what the trip meant, or what the future held for them; she was going to enjoy the present. She was heading to Maui with the man she loved, in his private jet aptly nicknamed *Adventure*.

Jada was thrilled, so ridiculously happy she thought her heart would burst. Forty-eight hours in paradise with her dream man? What could be better? What more could a girl want? The two-day trip was a once-in-a-lifetime opportunity, and Jada planned to make the most of her time alone with her suave, debonair crush. Confident they were going to have a magical, unforgettable weekend, Jada followed Max inside the waiting elevator, draped her arms around his neck and kissed him with such passion *her* knees buckled.

The interior of the Bombardier Challenger 850 Learjet was so sophisticated Jada was afraid to touch anything. She stood in the galley, fiddling with the turquoise bangle on her right hand. *Wow*, she thought, suddenly breathless. *So,* this *is how the other half lives!*

Jada admired her plush surroundings. Decked out in leather and gold accents, the private jet had a gleaming cabin, a spacious lounge and entertainment center, and a master bedroom with a king-size bed and a marble shower. Pillows and cushions were embossed with the Moore family crest, Waterford crystal lamps showered the space with light, and furnishings gave off an air of subtle luxury. Everyone in Max's family had access to the private plane to travel and to conduct business and on-site interviews, and since Jada handled all the bookings, she knew the Learjet was used on a weekly basis. It was popular with the Hollywood elite and the ultimate symbol of wealth among them, its cost running to millions of dollars.

"Max, this is a gorgeous aircraft." Jada had seen the plane from a distance several times before, but she'd never been inside the private jet, and was blown away by the opulence around her. "You sure know how to travel in style."

"Thanks, but if you think this is nice, wait until you see the Boeing 727 I ordered last month," he bragged. "It makes the interior of Air Force One look like a shuttle bus!"

A female voice came on over the intercom, greeting them in Spanish, then English, and Jada took a seat as instructed by the first officer. The air hostess, a slender brunette with dimpled cheeks, appeared in the cabin, offering drinks and snacks, but Jada was too nervous to eat. She hated flying, almost as much as she hated spiders, and clutched the armrest to stop herself from bolting from her seat. Max must have sensed her unease, because he reached out and clasped her hand. It helped. Her pulse slowed, and her limbs stopped shaking.

A cell phone rang, and hip-hop music filled the cabin. Max retrieved his iPhone from his pocket, then put it to his ear. Jada could tell by his furrowed brow that he was talking to an ex-lover or a disgruntled client, and decided she wasn't going to compete with his cell phone for his attention. In the past she had, but not tonight.

"Sorry about that," Max said, ending the call. "A client needed to vent, and I knew if I didn't answer she'd keep blowing up my cell, and that's the last thing I want."

His cell phone buzzed, but before he could answer it, Jada plucked it out of his hand. Thinking fast, she unzipped her purse, dropped it inside and slid the clutch under her seat. Keeping her eyes straight ahead, fixed on the flat-screen TV mounted in the corner of the cabin, she pretended not to notice Max staring at her with a bewildered expression on his face.

"What are you doing?"

"Saving you from yourself." Jada voiced her concerns about him having his cell phone during the flight. "Do you want to spend time with me or your cell? Because if you want your iPhone I can grab a cab back to my place."

"Oh, no, you won't. For the next forty-eight hours, you're mine, all mine."

"Just forty-eight hours?" she joked, batting her eyelashes. "That's enough for you?"

Chuckling good-naturedly, Max kissed her cheek. "Only time will tell."

"I can't believe we're flying to Hawaii right now. This is crazy!"

"No, what's crazy is that you've worked with me for years, but we've never traveled together. If you ask me, this trip is long overdue." His eyes dimmed, and the smile faded from his lips. "We have to head back to LA on Monday night, so we won't have much time for sightseeing, but can definitely squeeze in a private tour before we leave the island."

Baby, I don't care what we do or where we go, as long as we're together.

"What time does Wendell's party start?" Jada asked, curious about the event.

Max chuckled. "It started on Friday, and Sunday's the grand finale."

"A three-day birthday bash? I've never heard of such a thing. How indulgent."

"It's the latest celebrity trend, and I've attended several weeklong events for my other clients. If not for the Prescott George holiday mixer, I would have left for Maui days earlier."

"I've always wanted to visit Maui, but I haven't had the opportunity. What's it like?"

"Tranquil, stunning and picturesque,"he explained, reclining in his window seat. Clasping his hands on his stomach, he crossed his legs at the ankles as if he was relaxing in a hammock, and spoke in a soothing voice. "I love the locals, the traditional cuisine and culture, but I could do without the mosquitoes, the obnoxious tourists and the suffocating heat."

The jet climbed in the sky, high above the trees and clouds, but Jada was too busy chatting with Max about his favorite travel destinations to notice the view. His carefree attitude put her at ease, and his jokes made her shriek with laughter.

Yawning, Jada kicked off her shoes and closed her eyes. Seated comfortably in her leather armchair, she listened as Max recounted his most memorable Christmas, but she must have dozed off in the middle of his story, because the next thing Jada knew, he was urging her to wake up.

"Beautiful, it's time to get up. The plane just landed in Maui…"

Jada opened her eyes. Peering over his shoulder, she saw clear blue skies, radiant sunshine and sprawling fields of lush green grass. *I still can't believe it! I'm in Maui with Max!* Her temperature soared and excitement shot through her veins.

"We're here," Max announced, kissing the tip of her nose. "Let the adventures begin!"

Chapter 15

The outdoor lounge at the Four Seasons in Maui at Wailea was filled with so many magicians, clowns, hula dancers and men on stilts that Max thought he was at a summer carnival. The air smelled of popcorn and cotton candy, and although he'd enjoyed a delicious five-course lunch with Jada at one of the upscale restaurants in the hotel, the aroma tickling his nose made his mouth wet. Sweat spilled down his face, clinging to his short-sleeve Ralph Lauren dress shirt. Max needed an ice-cold drink, but held off from ordering a vodka tonic until after he found the guest of honor and wished him a happy birthday.

He stood beside the concession stand, holding Jada close to his side with one hand and a birthday gift for Wendell Coleman in the other. Max scanned the grounds for his favorite client, but he couldn't find the award-winning actor anywhere. Guests had honored the actor's request by wearing red, and the eight-tier birthday cake was the same vibrant shade. Max wanted to call Wendell to find out where he was, but remembered he'd left his iPhone in the suite to appease Jada, and didn't feel like running upstairs to retrieve it.

"Aloha!" chirped a female voice. "Welcome to Maui, the land of promise, allure and adventure. Mr. Coleman is thrilled that you are here to celebrate his sixtieth birthday, and wants you to party the night away, so eat, drink, dance and be merry!"

A resort employee appeared, draped leis around their necks and disappeared into the crowd. *Wendell wasn't kidding about going all out for his party*, Max thought. He looked around the lounge area, noting all the A-list stars devouring caviar, sipping Cristal and snapping pictures. He knew from speaking to the Chicago native earlier in the week that the star had not only booked out the entire resort for his birthday bash, he'd also spent millions of dollars on the event, and the costumes, decor and elaborate food stations were jaw-dropping. With over one hundred films to his credit, Wendell was known and loved worldwide, and Max felt fortunate to be his agent.

Sweating profusely, Max took the handkerchief out of his back pocket and wiped his forehead. Beside him, Jada swiveled her hips to the chart-topping reggae song the female DJ was spinning in her booth. The music was loud, the drinks were flowing, and guests clad in bikinis, swim trunks and evening wear were mingling, laughing and dancing. Photographers scrambled around the lounge, on the hunt for the perfect shot.

Spotting the gift box beside the bar, Max strode through the lounge, smiling and nodding at everyone he passed. He'd been to hundreds of five-star resorts in his life, but he was impressed by the natural beauty of the sprawling property, and decided this would be the first of many visits to the Four Seasons in Maui. Palm trees waved in the breeze, tropical flowers perfumed the air and ocean views created a tranquil ambience. Cabanas outfitted with plasma-screen TVs, chaise lounges and ceiling fans surrounded the infinity pool, and once Max dropped off Wendell's birthday gift he was going to relax inside the private cabana he'd reserved.

Dark gray clouds covered the sky, but the air was hot and stifling. Birds chirped, bees buzzed and insects flew around the lounge, annoying guests. Max put the gift in the oversize box, asked Jada what she wanted to drink and placed their orders with the silver-haired bartender with the jovial disposition.

Whistles, cheers and applause filled the lounge, seizing Max's attention. Glancing over his shoulder, he smiled at the guests on the field. Wendell had thought of everything, including old-school carnival games, and partyers were having so much fun playing Bean Bag Toss, Balloon Pop and Disk Drop that Max considered joining them. But he didn't want to leave Jada. They'd been inseparable since arriving at the resort hours earlier, and Max knew if he left her alone at the bar someone would swoop in and steal his place. Like that afternoon, when he'd stepped out of the hotel gift shop to take a phone call from Taylor. He'd returned five minutes later, to find a musician with Lenny Kravitz hair putting the moves on Jada. She'd laughed, insisted he had nothing to worry about, but Max didn't want to take any chances where she was concerned. Stunning in a flower-printed sundress and caged sandals, Jada attracted male attention everywhere she went, and Max didn't want to lose her to one of the celebrity guests.

"I haven't played Ring Toss since I was a kid." Entering their private cabana, Max sat down on the tan couch, put his feet up on the coffee table and tasted his drink. "My parents used to take me and Bianca to Six Flags practically every weekend, and we'd spend hours on the rides, playing games and goofing off."

"Lucky you. I've never been to Six Flags, or any other amusement park."

"Really?" he asked, surprised by her admission. Though Jada had worked closely with him for two years, and knew all about his personal life, Max didn't know much about her upbringing. He wanted to learn more. "But Six Flags is literally right in your backyard. It's practically a national treasure, and every kid's dream vacation."

"I wanted to go, but money was always tight for my family, and I didn't want to make my dad feel bad by asking him to take me somewhere I knew he couldn't afford…"

Listening to Jada open up about her family and the sacrifices she'd made over the years for them made Max feel close to her. She told him about her broken home, her estranged relationship with her mom and her younger siblings. Max couldn't think of a time when he wasn't attracted to bad girls, women who liked breaking the rules and living on the edge, but he was moved by Jada's sincerity and admired her even more. She charmed him with her childhood stories, made him smile and chuckle. They sat in the cabana, talking, flirting and kissing, oblivious to everyone else at the party, and if not for the deafening applause that erupted in the lounge, Max wouldn't have noticed Wendell, or the mammoth five-ton elephant he rode in on.

Max got up and stood in front of the cabana, watching the actor's grand entrance. Impressed, he couldn't figure out how Wendell had pulled it off, but cheered when his client took center stage. His salt-and-pepper hair gave him a dapper look, his slim-fitted cherry-red suit was eye-catching, and his diamond jewelry complemented his flashy designer ensemble.

The DJ lowered the music, then handed Wendell the microphone.

"Thanks for coming, everyone!" Wendell smiled and waved. "I figured I should get to my party before everyone gets wasted and forgets why they traveled to Maui in the first place!"

Hearty chuckles and snickers rippled through the crowd. The female drummer banged the cymbals, drawing another cheer from the guests, and Wendell flashed a thumbs-up. Despite his staggering fame and fortune, he'd never forgotten his roots, and spoke with warmth and humility about his friends and loved ones.

"None of this would be possible without my soul mate, my ride-or-die for the past nineteen years, Norchelle." Wendell wrapped his arms around his statuesque, dark-skinned wife, kissed the top of her head, then her lips. "Thanks for everything you do for me, our family, and for being the best wife a man could ever ask for…"

Max finished his drink. He was moved by the actor's heartfelt speech. And he wasn't the only one. Jada sniffed, then dabbed at the corners of her eyes with her fingertips. Max draped an arm around her waist. His hands wanted to explore her body, one delectable inch at a time, but he reminded himself they were in public and exercised self-control.

"All this talk about love and happiness is putting me in the mood…"

Max cranked his head to the right and stared at Jada

with wide eyes. He'd never seen this side of her—the bold, provocative temptress with the sultry bed-me voice—and it made him wonder what other secrets the petite beauty was keeping from him.

Leaning in close, Jada brushed her lips against his ear. "Shall we go?"

Lust infected his body, shooting through his veins, and seconds passed before his thoughts cleared. Max hadn't been intimate with anyone in months, not since his dad's dire cancer prognosis, and he couldn't think of anything better than making love to Jada. Max knew the answer to the question in his thoughts, but he asked it anyways. "Go where?"

"Back to your suite, of course. Or mine, if you prefer. It doesn't matter to me."

"Let me touch base with Wendell first. I can't come all this way and not wish him a happy birthday," he explained, kissing her cheek. "You understand, don't you, baby?"

Smirking, her eyes bright with mischief, Jada held a hand in the air and wiggled her long, slender fingers. "You have five minutes, then that ass is mine."

Max erupted in laughter, chuckled long and hard for several seconds at her joke. *That ass is mine?* Why did her bold, unexpected quip turn him on? Max studied Jada closely, noted her glassy eyes and flirtatious demeanor. She was tipsy. No doubt about it. Max prided himself on being a gentleman, and decided he'd be going to bed alone tonight. It wasn't the end of the world. They could make love in the morning, before their private tour, or when they returned to LA on Monday night. As long as Jada didn't catch feelings, they'd have one hell of a holiday fling, and Max was looking forward to every erotic minute of it.

A slide show filled with memorable moments of Wendell's life played on a projector, and guests oohed and aahed during the twenty-minute video. The cake was cut, dozens of speeches were made, and celebrity performers rocked the stage. Wendell worked the resort lounge with the charm and charisma of Obama, and when the actor threw his arms around Max and kissed his cheek, everyone standing nearby chuckled. "You made it! Good to see you, Max."

"There's the man of the hour," Max said, with a broad grin. "Happy birthday, man."

"Thanks, son, and who's this lovely lady beside you with the beautiful smile?"

Before Max could speak, Jada introduced herself to Wendell and told him she was touched by his speech about his wife and their marriage. "You were brilliant, Mr. Coleman."

Smoke curled up from Wendell's cigar as he spoke. "Son, I like her. She's smart, has good taste and a *great* ear. Wife her!"

"Been there, done that, and I'm not doing it again," Max said, with a laugh.

"Spoken like a true player." Wendell clapped Max on the shoulder. "Just wait. Your time will come. You'll find love when you least expect it, and when you do, it will knock you clear off your feet, but you'll be a better man because of it."

Max didn't respond, but the expression on his face must have revealed his disbelief, because Wendell continued, full steam ahead, imparting words of wisdom.

"I've been divorced twice, and swore up and down that I'd never get married again, but the moment I met Norchelle, I was a goner. Done. All in."

His gaze found his wife in the crowd, and a proud smile exploded across his face.

"Do you know what sealed my fate? How I knew Norchelle was The One?"

"No," Jada said in a breathless tone of voice. "What did she do?"

Her eyes were wide and bright, filled with wonder, and Max knew Jada was loving the actor's story. A small crowd gathered around them, and he groaned inwardly, wished they didn't have an audience listening in. Like most actors, Wendell loved being the center of attention—and hearing his own voice—and once he started yapping about his wife and kids there was just no stopping him.

"Days after we met, I got pneumonia and was hospitalized. Norchelle never left my side. She fed me soup, read me comics, and cursed me out every time I snapped at one of the nurses." Wendell laughed at the memory. "Norchelle keeps it real with me, no matter what, and loves me without fail, even when I screw up. Proposing on our third date was the smartest thing I've ever done, and I've never once regretted my decision."

"Liar!" Max joked, cocking an eyebrow. "That's not real life. That's the script for your new romantic comedy on BET, and you know it!"

Everyone laughed. Guests wanted to know more about the TV show, but Max was done shooting the breeze with Wendell. Had had enough of his advice for one day. He didn't want the actor to put crazy thoughts in Jada's head, and knew if they stuck around, listening to him preach about the benefits of marriage, it would ruin his good mood.

"Norchelle is my one true love," Wendell continued in an awe-filled voice. "And I wouldn't be the man I am today without her unconditional love and unwavering support. She's the reason for my every success, and I owe everything I am to her."

Mrs. Coleman appeared, with a photographer in tow, and linked arms with her husband. "Max, you don't mind if I borrow my husband for a minute, do you? I'll bring him right back."

Grateful for the interruption, Max nodded and said, "No worries, Norchelle. He's all yours!" Giving Wendell a fist bump, he promised to touch base with him next week, then escorted Jada through the lounge, into the hotel lobby and to the waiting elevator before the guest of honor could stop them from leaving the party.

Chapter 16

"Max, what can I get you to drink?" Jada asked, un-locking the door to her hotel suite. She turned on the floor lamp and dropped her key card on the chestnut-brown table against the wall. Her cell phone buzzed from inside her clutch purse, but Jada ignored it. Didn't want any distractions while she was with Max, wanted to give him her undivided attention—and more. He'd been quiet in the elevator, hadn't said much when she'd asked him what his plans were for New Year's Eve, and appeared to be deep in thought. "I'm going to grab a raspberry wine cooler from the minibar. Do you want one?"

Her question was met by silence. Jada glanced over her shoulder, saw Max standing in the hallway instead of inside her suite and frowned. Couldn't understand what he was doing, and why he was dodging her gaze. "You're not coming in?"

Stepping back, he stuffed his hands into the front pockets of his khakis and jingled the coins inside. "No. It's late, and we have a full day ahead of us tomorrow. The private island tour starts at seven a.m., and if I want to be alert I need a full night's sleep."

Jada didn't laugh at his joke. He was lying. It was only nine o'clock, much too early for a party animal like Max to retire for the night. Having been his assistant for years, Jada knew that he didn't go to bed until midnight or later, and was awake and raring to go every morning by the crack of dawn.

Questions overwhelmed her mind. *Is he meeting up with someone else?* Slanting her head to the right, Jada studied his face for signs of deception. Had he made a connection with one of the female celebrities at the party? Was that why he was anxious to leave? They'd been joined at the hip since arriving at the resort that morning, and he'd scarcely used his cell phone, but that didn't mean he hadn't made late-night plans with someone else. Instead of wondering what was going on, Jada asked, "Max, what's wrong? I thought we were having fun."

Seconds passed, lasted so long that Jada realized he wasn't going to answer the question. She didn't understand why he was suddenly giving her the cold shoulder. They'd had a great day together—hanging out at the resort, eating delicious food, chatting about their hobbies and interests for hours—and making love inside her suite would be the perfect end to a perfect date. For once, his cell phone wasn't ringing or buzzing off the hook, and having his undivided attention made Jada feel special, as if he cared about her and wanted to make her happy. And he had. He'd been a perfect gentleman since they'd arrived in Hawaii, and Jada wanted to create more wonderful memories with him. Being on his arm was a thrill, and she'd enjoyed meeting his celebrity friends at Wendell Coleman's birthday bash, but the highlight of their trip was hanging out in the private cabana, talking and kissing.

Hearing a pop, Jada glanced around the suite for the source of the noise. Her gaze strayed to the balcony window. Fireworks lit up the night sky, and the dazzling display brought a smile to her lips. *Wendell Coleman sure knows how to party!*

"It's nothing personal," Max said quietly. "You're tipsy, and I don't want you to wake up in the morning and hate me for taking advantage of you."

Please do! Jada had never heard anything more absurd, but instead of rolling her eyes she tried to soothe his fears. "Max, I won't. Furthermore, I'm not tipsy. I feel great!" To prove it, she walked toward him in a straight line, reciting the alphabet. "See! I *told* you I wasn't drunk."

"I still don't think it's a good idea I come in, so I'll see you tomorrow. Good night."

Max turned to leave, but Jada grabbed his arm and pulled him inside her suite. "Not so fast." Determined to have her way, and her man, she said, "I'm not ready for you to go."

Slamming the door shut with the back of her foot, she set her sights on Max.

"What now?" He looked amused, as if he was trying not to laugh. "You're in control."

Desire consumed her. It was so strong and powerful Jada couldn't fight it, and did what she'd been fantasizing about for years. What she'd been dreaming of doing from the moment she'd first laid eyes on him. Kissing him hard on the mouth, with every ounce of passion coursing through her veins, Jada ripped his shirt from his body and caressed his broad, muscled chest with her hands. Stroked his shoulders. Rubbed his nipples. Licked and sucked his earlobe into her mouth. "You feel amazing," she purred, her voice a breathless whisper. "Don't worry. We won't do anything you're not comfortable with. I promise."

"Hey, that's *my* line!"

Laughing and kissing, they stumbled through the suite and collapsed onto the king-size bed. The lights were low, perfect for lovemaking, and classical music was playing in the distance, adding to the romantic ambience in the room. Max took his time undressing her, and Jada reveled in his touch. She loved feeling his mouth against hers, on her neck and shoulders, and giggled when he flicked his tongue against her ears. Pleasure engulfed her body. Her nipples hardened, and her sex tingled.

Max cupped her breasts in his hands. Jada cried out. Begged him for more. Told him to do it again. Moaned to the heavens when he obliged. Her blood pressure spiked, causing the room to spin around her, and Jada feared she was going to pass out. His lips were against her mouth, his hands were in her hair, then between her legs, turning her out with each flick of his long, deft fingers.

Jada sucked in a breath. Every inch of her body was throbbing with need, desperate for him. His fingers played in her curls, parted her fleshy lips, then swirled inside her sex. In and out, back and forth, each move more explosive than the last. Electricity singed her skin, and moans tumbled off her lips. Her throat was hoarse, and her body was on fire, scalding hot. *I'm going to explode, and he isn't even inside me yet!*

To regain the upper hand, Jada rolled on top of Max and pinned his hands above his head. Pressing soft, featherlight kisses along his collarbone and torso, she told him how handsome he was. His body was perfect, flawless, and exploring his chiseled physique with her tongue and hands was the most thrilling experience of her life. "This is amazing... *You're* amazing, and I can't get enough of you..."

Her appetite for him was insatiable, and the longer they kissed and caressed each other's bodies, the harder it was for Jada to control her emotions. She started to tell Max the truth, that she loved him with all her heart, but when he gazed deep into her eyes she got cold feet. Was scared that if she did he'd lose interest in her, and Jada didn't want to chase him off. In one night, they'd gone from zero to one hundred, but she'd been dreaming about this moment for years, and wanted to experience the pleasure of his lovemaking. Couldn't imagine a better Christmas gift.

"What are you doing to me? I've never felt this way before..." His voice was husky, filled with desperation, and it was the sexiest thing Jada had ever heard. An orgasm for her ears. Feeling powerful, as if she could do anything she wanted, she unbuckled his pants, yanked down his zipper and slid a hand inside his boxer briefs.

Pleasure shot straight to her core. Her mouth watered and her heart thumped at the sight of his erection—long, wide and ridiculously thick. She wanted it between her legs, and she shivered uncontrollably at the thought. Jada stroked his shaft until it was good and hard.

Facing him, she watched his eyes roll in the back of his head, his lips part, and heard a groan fall from his mouth. He cradled her head in his hands, holding her in place, giving her a rush. Jada knew what he wanted, what he needed, and answered his unspoken request.

To please him, she lowered her head to his lap, gripped his erection and sucked it into her mouth. Swirled her tongue around it. Licked the length. Tickled and nibbled the tip. Stroked it with her hands. That morning, while waiting in the lobby for Max to arrange their private island tour with the front desk clerk, she'd flipped through the January issue of *Cosmopolitan* magazine. Recalling the sizzling sex tips she'd read, Jada decided to put the article to the test. Increasing her pace, she sucked his erection harder, faster, and moved her body in a sensual way, rubbing her breasts against his skin.

Max groaned, then cursed in Spanish, and Jada knew she was doing something right. She was emboldened by his praise, and her confidence grew. She'd never had sex before, let alone made the first move on a guy, but calling the shots in the bedroom made her feel fierce, invincible, more ballsy than Wonder Woman. Jada liked how he tasted, enjoyed pleasing him, and varied her pressure and speed to excite him. It worked. Max pulled her to his chest and kissed her passionately on the mouth, stealing her breath for the second time in minutes.

"You're something else, you know that?" Kissing the corner of her lips, he tenderly stroked her cheeks with the back of his hand. "Are you sure this is what you want?"

Jada nodded her head. "Yes. I want you to be my first."

The grin slid off his face.

"Come again?" His voice carried a note of confusion. "*What* did you just say?"

"I'm a virgin, and you're the only man I want to make love to."

Max sat up, then shot to his feet.

Panic seized her heart. "What's wrong? Where are you going?"

"I shouldn't be here. This is a mistake."

"No, it's not. I want this, Max. I want you."

Max grabbed his clothes off the floor, put them on, then dragged a hand down the length of his face. "Your first time should be special, with someone who's a hundred percent committed to you, not a casual hookup in Maui that doesn't mean anything."

Is that what this is? A casual hookup that doesn't mean anything to you? Something broke inside her, causing her spirits to sink and her heart to ache. Crushed by his words, she felt her eyes tear up, but Jada willed herself not to cry. Didn't want Max to know his confession was a blow to her self-esteem. Jada snatched a pillow off the bed and covered her naked body. Five minutes ago, she'd been all over him, and now she just wanted Max to leave her suite.

"You're an incredible woman, and I think the world of you, but I don't want a serious relationship," Max said, his smile apologetic.

Ice spread through her veins, chilling her to the bone, but Jada governed her temper. Didn't lash out at him. She'd been fooling herself. This wasn't her. Sex without love was meaningless, and even though she wanted him to be her first, she had to protect her heart. Max was right: she deserved better. As much as she loved him, she loved herself more, and wanted a relationship, not a Christmas fling. One day, she'd meet the right man who'd be worthy of her, and it saddened her that it wasn't Max.

"This is wrong… I shouldn't have come here… I don't know what I was thinking…"

The desk phone rang, and Max broke off speaking.

"Aren't you going to answer it? It could be important."

Shaking her head, Jada lowered her gaze to the carpet as she searched the room for her dress and undergarments. Finding them, she snatched them off the couch, put them on and made a beeline for the bathroom. Jada caught sight of her reflection in the wall mirror and cringed. Wished she could click her heels three times and return to LA. Her hair was sticking up, mascara was smeared across her cheeks, and her outfit was a wrinkled mess. Jada wanted to hide out in the bathroom until Max was gone, but when his voice cracked she stopped dead in her tracks.

"Derek, talk to me," he demanded, shouting into the receiver. "What happened?"

Jada spun around, facing him. Seeing the tension in his jaw, she feared something bad had happened to Taylor while she was with her mom. Was the tween in trouble? Had she been hurt?

Pushing her feelings aside, Jada approached the desk and placed a hand on Max's shoulder. She wanted him to know she was there for him, if he needed her. And it was obvious he did. Hanging his head, he wiped at his eyes with the back of his hand. Jada was hurt that he'd rejected her, but she wanted to comfort him. Ending the call, Max dropped the phone in the cradle and kicked the desk chair so hard it fell over with a thud.

"What's wrong? What happened?"

Closing his eyes, he took a deep breath and raked a hand through his short black hair. "My dad collapsed this afternoon and was rushed to the hospital. He's stable now, and my brothers were able to take him home, but doctors don't think he'll make it through the night."

"Max, I am so sorry. Reginald looked great last night at the holiday mixer, and I thought his health had improved."

"We all did, but his supposed breakthrough was false hope. He's dying, and there's nothing anyone can do about it." Max crossed the room, unlocked the adjoining door and yanked it open. "I'm going to call Captain Woodson, and let her know our plans have changed. I'll be back to get you in ten minutes, so please be ready to go."

Max left, slamming the door behind him, and Jada leaned against the couch. Her heart broke for him. His father was dying, his business rival was gunning for him, and he was having problems with his daughter. No wonder he didn't want a serious relationship. He had enough on his plate, and Jada didn't want to be a burden to him, a nuisance like all the other women in his past who wouldn't take no for an answer.

Reality struck, and her thoughts cleared. It was time for her to face the truth, to stop pretending she could have a successful relationship with Max one day. Sure, they had great conversations about life, and shared morals and values, but they weren't meant to be, and she needed to move on. His well-being was no longer her concern, and once they returned to LA she had to distance herself from him. They were over, and she had to put the past behind her.

Tomorrow, she'd contact Shazir and accept his job

offer. Why not? It was a great opportunity, with a fantastic agency, and she'd be a fool to turn it down. Her mind made up, Jada stood, grabbed her hand luggage from the closet and hurled clothes, shoes and beauty products inside.

Chapter 17

On Thursday afternoon, Max sat beside Reginald at the round walnut-brown table inside the boardroom at the Prescott George headquarters, hoping for his dad's sake that Demetrius would show up for the emergency meeting that had been scheduled for two o'clock. The committee had planned to gather on Monday, to discuss the San Diego sabotage case with all parties involved, but Demetrius had canceled at the last minute. All week, he'd been giving them the runaround, claiming he had the stomach flu one day, a migraine the next, and car trouble yesterday, but Max didn't believe him. Demetrius would do anything to avoid facing Reginald and the board members. Tired of the businessman's games, his brothers had offered to pick him up at his Malibu mansion and agreed to personally escort him to the conference room.

To pass the time, Reginald chatted with the board members. His speech was slow, and talking seemed to require all the strength he had, but he joked around with his long-time friends. Max had a lot on his mind, and couldn't stop his thoughts from racing, but he listened to the conversation, nodding in agreement as his dad reminisced about the past. Despite his failing health, Reginald was in a good mood, and listening to his father crack jokes made Max realize all hope wasn't lost. His dad was still alive, and he was going to cherish every moment they had together.

"Seriously, Reginald, how are you keeping?" a media mogul asked with a sad smile.

"It's true what they say. You can't keep a good man down. Or quiet!"

A software company CEO, with a thick mustache, spoke in a jovial voice. "I believe you, old friend. I haven't seen you this lively since you won a million at the Bellagio in '09. Blackjack always was your game, and I bet you still have a hot hand."

"That was one hell of a weekend." A pensive expression covered Reginald's gaunt face. "To be honest, it's a blur in my mind. I drank a whole *lot* of tequila that night, and so did you!"

Chuckles filled the air as Reginald bumped fists with his friends.

Max drummed his fingers on the table. Pulling back the sleeve of his navy Tom Ford suit jacket, he glanced at his diamond watch. Demetrius was thirty minutes late for the meeting, and hadn't even had the decency to call and explain his tardiness to the group.

Max cursed under his breath. *You've* got *to be kidding me*, he fumed, gripping the armrest of his leather chair. *Who does Demetrius think he is? The Donald? Why is he jerking us around? Doesn't he realize this is a matter of life and death?*

Struggling to control his temper, Max took his cell

phone out of his jacket pocket and typed in his password. Staring at his screensaver—a selfie he'd taken with Jada at Wendell Coleman's birthday party—brought cherished memories to mind. He tried not to think about their romantic weekend in Maui, but it was a losing battle.

Images of her bombarded his thoughts. The fact that Jada was a virgin who wanted him to be her first lover made him desire her even more. Made him realize how special she was. She was his rock, the only person besides his father whom he could count on, and Max missed seeing her around the office. And venting to her about his problems. He hadn't spoken to Jada since they'd returned to LA on Monday, and although he longed to hear her voice, he couldn't bring himself to call her. Not after the way he'd treated her in Maui. There was no doubt in his mind that she wanted nothing to do with him, and he didn't want to upset her.

His thoughts returned to yesterday's staff meeting, and pain stabbed his heart. He'd learned from one of his employees that Jada had accepted a full-time position as Shazir's personal assistant, and trolling the talent scout's social-media pages had confirmed it. Shazir had bragged about his gorgeous new hire online, making Max feel even worse for his behavior in Hawaii, but it was too late to apologize. He had to move on. He wished her well, but he hated the idea of her working for his rival. Even worse, Jada had cut ties with Taylor, and his daughter was devastated. Max told her not to worry, reminded her that she had friends and family who loved her, but nothing he said made Taylor feel better. That afternoon, she'd called as he was driving to the Prescott George headquarters, upset because Jada wasn't answering her texts or phone calls. Hearing his daughter cry broke his heart, but Jada had made her decision, and even though Max didn't agree with it, he had to respect it.

The conference room door flew open, and Demetrius shuffled inside, wearing a gray fedora, wrinkled golf attire and a long face. Trey and Derek followed behind him, sat down at the table and nodded at Max. Anxious to get the meeting started, Max put his cell phone on the table, cleared his throat and addressed the board members.

"My brothers and I requested this emergency meeting to not only prove my dad had nothing to do with what happened to the San Diego chapter, but that he was framed by his oldest and dearest friend, Demetrius Davis." Max reached into his brown leather satchel at the foot of his chair and searched for the manila folder. It was the smoking gun, the information he'd searched months for, and thanks to the private investigator he'd hired, he finally had the documentation he needed to clear his father's name. From the detailed report, he'd learned that the computer leaks and viruses that had affected the San Diego chapter had originated from a server in Demetrius's office.

And that wasn't all. He'd tracked down Demetrius's ex-wife, Ellen Davis, in nearby San Bernardino, and met with the soft-spoken mother of three on Tuesday afternoon. Ellen had told Max everything he needed to know about her vindictive ex-husband. After Demetrius learned about Ellen's affair with Reginald, he'd vowed to get even during the divorce proceedings and had made good on his threat. He'd seen to it that Ellen was ostracized by their friends and had told their adult daughters about the affair. What he'd uncovered about the celebrated businessman was mind-blowing, more shocking than an episode of *Scandal*, and every salacious word of the five-page report was true. Max was angry about what Demetrius had done to Ellen and Reginald, but a small part of him felt bad for the businessman. Reginald had not only broken the Bro Code, he'd humiliated the man he called his Brother, and nothing his dad ever said or did would alleviate Demetrius's pain.

Unable to find the folder, Max dumped the satchel on the table. He searched through his things, but it wasn't there. He scratched his head. Where could it be? That morning, when Christina stopped by his office to discuss the Prescott George Christmas Eve charity fund-raiser, he'd taken the folder out of his desk and put it in his satchel. Had he misplaced it? Accidentally left it in his office? Max didn't know where the document was and hoped his screwup wouldn't affect his dad's case.

"Find what you're looking for, son?" Demetrius asked with a crooked grin.

Max could smell his arrogance, his pride, and suspected that Demetrius had something to do with the missing document. Choosing to dwell on the positives, not the negatives, he abandoned his search for the folder, clasped his hands in front of him and addressed the balding businessman. "I had a document detailing your involvement in the San Diego sabotage case, but unfortunately, it's gone missing. Thankfully, I have Ellen's cell number. Should I call her, or do you want to man up and come clean about what you did to my father?"

The grin slid off Demetrius's face, and panic flashed in his eyes.

"Demetrius, is this true?" a board member asked, stroking his salt-and-pepper goatee. "Are you responsible for the break-ins, computer leaks and vandalism that plagued the San Diego chapter last summer? Were you angry at Reginald, and framed him to take the fall?"

"This is your last chance. Tell us the truth, or I'm calling your ex-wife." To loosen Demetrius's tongue, and prove he was serious about his threat, Max grabbed his cell phone off the table, accessed his Contacts app and searched for Ellen's number. "I'll put her on speakerphone, so everyone can hear what she has to say about your bitter quest for revenge."

"No! Don't!" Demetrius shot to his feet, mumbling under his breath as he paced the length of the sun-filled conference room. Max couldn't make out what he was saying, but his hunched shoulders, woeful disposition and teary voice said it all: he was guilty.

"Tell us what you did. This is important." Trey stood. He joined Demetrius in front of the window and placed a hand on his shoulder. "My dad is dying, and you owe it to me and my brothers to tell us what happened."

"Reginald is ill, and we want to clear his name before he…" Unable to finish his thought, Derek broke off speaking and hung his head. "Do the right thing, Demetrius—"

"I did it! It's true! I admit it!" Demetrius shouted.

Silence fell across the room.

"I was angry about the affair, and I wanted to get even!" Demetrius fell into an armchair, took off his iron-rimmed eyeglasses and dropped his face in his palms. "I just wanted Reginald to suffer and get kicked out of the organization he loved so much, but I never meant for the San Diego chapter to suffer, or for the LA chapter to get a six-month suspension. That was never my intention…"

Relief flowed through Max, but he stared at Demetrius with disgust. He couldn't believe the man who'd been like a second father to him could be so vindictive and mean.

"I... I—I didn't think something like that would happen," Demetrius continued, his voice wobbling with emotion. "I messed up, and I'm sincerely sorry about the trouble I caused."

Demetrius broke down then, cried so hard his shoulders shook, and his deep, racking sobs filled the air. Reginald rolled his wheelchair across the room, spoke in a quiet voice, just loud enough for the disgraced businessman to hear, and clapped him on the back.

"Reginald, man, I'm sorry about what I did. Can you find it in your heart to forgive me?"

"Of course I can. You're not the only one who's made mistakes. I've done some pretty messed-up things in my life, and if Trey and Derek can forgive me for being a pitiful excuse for a father when they were kids, then I can forgive you, too."

Blown away by his father's speech, Max stared at Reginald with wide eyes. Like his brothers, he'd loved Demetrius deeply, but he was disappointed about the spiteful things he'd done. Max didn't know if he'd ever be able to forgive him. Maybe in time, but not today. Not until he answered for what he'd done to Reginald. Board members, still reeling from Demetrius's confession, looked bewildered.

"What happens now?" Demetrius wiped at his cheeks. "What is my punishment?"

Heads bent, board members spoke quietly for several seconds.

"You owe restitution to both the San Diego and Los Angeles chapters," the committee chairman announced in a stern voice. "Effective immediately, your membership has been indefinitely revoked. We wish we could keep this ugly situation quiet and deal with it in-house, but we have no choice but to contact the authorities. You broke the law, and you have to answer for what you did in San Diego…"

Max glanced down at the table, saw his cell phone light up and stared at the number on the screen. A groan rose in his throat. He didn't want to talk to Shay. Not now. They'd argued days earlier about Taylor going on a "date" with TaVonte to a Sunday matinee movie, and their conversation had left a bitter taste in his mouth. Max didn't understand why his ex-wife was going out of her way to piss him off, and he was sick of her appeasing Taylor. These days, his daughter was acting like a spoiled brat who thought she didn't have to listen to her father. Max knew Taylor was upset that Jada was out of their lives, but that was no excuse for her behavior. Max thought of letting the call go to voice mail, but knew that if he did, Shay would ream him out for being an absentee father, and he didn't feel like hearing her complain.

Wanting privacy, Max grabbed his phone off the table, then exited the conference room. "Shay, what is it? I'm in the middle of an important meeting, and I can't talk."

Deep, racking sobs filled the line, and Max feared his ex-wife had lost her mother. Yesterday, when he'd talked to Taylor, she'd mentioned that her grandma Virginia was back in the hospital due to complications from surgery. "Shay, I am so sorry—"

"You should be!" she snapped. "Taylor is missing, and it's all your fault. I'll *never* forgive you if something bad happens to my baby girl."

Her words didn't register, didn't add up in his mind. "What did you just say?"

"I came to pick her up from school, but she's not here, and no one knows where she is."

Max felt a sinking feeling in his stomach and a painful sensation in his chest.

"I… I—I can't lose her," Shay stammered. "Taylor's my world, and I love her more than anything. She's the best thing that's ever happened to me."

He asked her to speak to school officials, but Shay was too emotional to do what he asked.

"Wh-wh-what if she's been kidnapped? What if someone took my baby?"

"Shay, don't talk like that." Charging toward the elevator, Max noticed the time on the wall clock as he took his car keys out of his pocket. He refused to think the worst. School had ended ten minutes earlier, and Max was convinced there was a good reason for his daughter's absence. "I'm on my way. Don't move. We'll find her. I swear."

"You better, and when we do we're going to court to revise our custody agreement."

His heart dropped, and his car keys fell from his hands. Max tried to speak, but he didn't have the words. He wanted to find his daughter, not argue with his ex-wife.

"I'm going to fight for sole custody to protect Taylor, from the emotional roller coaster of being *your* child," she spit. "You're the problem, Max, and I won't let you hurt her again."

His vision blurred, and fear knotted inside his chest. Max had only cried three times in his life: the morning his mother had died at UCLA Medical Center, the day Taylor was born and the night Reginald had revealed

Max disagreed. "It's only been thirty minutes. Let's keep looking. I *know* she's here somewhere…"

Jada entered the office and noticed a large group of people gathered around the front desk, arguing. Max was there with his brothers, school administration officials and a short, stocky man she didn't recognize. The stranger, dressed in a Dodgers baseball cap and navy coveralls, stood behind Shay, and it was obvious by the way he was touching her that they were a couple. Young and fashionable, with a wardrobe that could rival a Grammy-winning pop star's, Shay was always well put together, but today the single mom had tearstained cheeks, a runny nose and a crooked ponytail.

"Jada? What are you doing here?"

At the sound of Max's voice, Jada nodded in greeting and forced a smile. Tried not to let her nervousness show, even though her palms were damp and her knees were knocking together. As usual, he smelled delicious and looked handsome in his tailored suit, silk tie and polished shoes. Days had passed with no word from him, and although they'd never be a couple or work together again, she'd longed to talk to him. To laugh and joke around like they used to. Memories of Max and Taylor were never far from her thoughts, but for her own sanity she had to move on with her life, even though every day without them made her feel worse.

Staring down at her leggings, she shifted her sneaker-clad feet and tugged at the sleeve of her sweatshirt. She wished she'd had time to shower and change before driving to the school, but Shay had called her in a panic while Jada was working out with Aubree and Delilah at LA Fitness, and she'd grabbed her bag and left without any thought to her appearance.

"I called her," Shay answered, stepping forward.

"Jada loves Taylor, too, and I thought she could help us find her. The more people looking for her, the better, right?"

"Yes, of course. Good thinking," Max said, slowly nodding his head.

"Thanks for coming, Jada. We really appreciate it." Holding a wad of Kleenex, Shay dabbed at her eyes, then blew her nose. "Taylor's classmates said she was in the band room at the end of the day, but we searched the entire building, with no luck. We checked out her favorite areas in the neighborhood, too, but came up empty. I don't know what else to do."

"Has anyone called TaVonte Williams?" Jada asked, thinking aloud. "He's her best friend, and if anyone will know where Taylor is, it's TaVonte. These days they're practically joined at the hip, and they like to hang out after school."

The vice principal stepped forward and shook his head. "Unfortunately, TaVonte was absent today. I spoke to his grandmother several minutes ago, and she explained that he's home sick with the flu."

Something hit the window, drawing Jada's gaze across the room. Students were playing soccer, and every time the ball hit the glass the group giggled. Noticing the man-made lake across the field, Jada remembered something Taylor had said weeks earlier, while they were having their pedicures done at the beauty salon. *There's a lake near my school, and TaVonte and I have lunch at our favorite bench every day... Sometimes we throw rocks into the lake and make wishes... Sometimes we listen to music or record videos...*

"We should check the lake," Jada said. "It's a long shot, but you never know."

"Y-y-you think Taylor's in there?" Shay stammered, her eyes wide with alarm.

"No, she might be there with some of her friends. It's her favorite hang-out spot."

Max touched her forearm. "Are you sure?"

Her thoughts scattered, but she found her voice. "It's just a hunch. I could be wrong, but it's worth checking out. We have nothing to lose."

Everyone filed out of the office and through the front door. Jada wanted to run across the field, shouting Taylor's name, but resisted the urge. Feeling guilty for not responding to the tween's earlier messages, she hoped her silence hadn't pushed Taylor to run away, and purposed in her heart to do something special for the fifth grader during the Christmas holidays.

"She's there!" Shay yelled, breaking out into a slow jog. "Taylor's wearing her school uniform, but I'd recognize her floral jean jacket anywhere!"

From where Jada was standing, she could see the bewildered expression on Taylor's face and hoped the tween wasn't mad at her for leading her parents to her secret hiding spot. Mother, father and daughter embraced. Then Max picked Taylor up off the ground and swung her in the air. One by one, everyone hugged Taylor, but when Jada waved at the tween, her gaze darkened.

Regret flooded Jada's body, making her feel low, but she smiled in greeting. "Hey, kiddo," she said, ignoring the painful knot in her throat. "How's it going?"

Shrugging, Taylor stared down at her black Mary Jane shoes. "Okay, I guess."

"Are you mad at me?"

"Not anymore." She kicked a rock across the field. "If you don't want to talk to me anymore, that's fine.

It's no big deal. I have lots of friends, and they think I'm great."

"You are, Taylor. You're the smartest, funniest fifth grader I know, and I love hanging out with you."

Hope sparked in Taylor's eyes, brightening her face. "You do?"

"Of course I do." Reaching out, Jada took Taylor's hand in her own and squeezed it. "If it's okay with your mom and dad, maybe we could go ice-skating this weekend. My treat. What do you say?"

Taylor cocked her head to the right and flashed a cheeky smile. "Throw in some cookie dough ice cream *and* a chocolate milkshake from Creams and Dreams, and you're on!"

Everyone laughed. Plans were made for the group to have dinner at a local restaurant, and as they started back across the field, Jada realized she'd made a huge mistake distancing herself from Taylor. *What's wrong with me? What was I thinking? How could I* not *be friends with the bubbly, fun-loving tween with the outrageous sense of humor?* That was like living without the sun, and just because she wasn't friends with Max didn't mean she shouldn't be friends with his daughter. Jada adored Taylor, and made up her mind to talk to Shay and Max about having a girls' day with the tween once a month.

"Jada, hold up." Max gripped her arm, then slid in front of her. "We need to talk."

Her mouth dried. Was he bothered by what she'd said to Taylor? Did he have a problem with her making plans with his daughter? Opposed to them spending time together? Jada didn't want to talk to Max, but he was blocking her path to the parking lot, and since she didn't want to cause a scene she decided to hear him out.

He had two minutes to say his piece, and that was it; she wasn't giving him a second more of her time. Tired and hungry, Jada wanted to go home and make dinner, not shoot the breeze with her former crush.

Former crush? repeated her inner voice. *Who are you kidding? You* still *love him!*

"You're incredible." His gaze and his tone were filled with awe. "You did it again."

Jada raised an eyebrow. "Did what?"

"Saved the day. I don't know how you do it, but you always say and do the right thing, and as usual you were bang on. Thank you for helping us find Taylor. We couldn't have done it without you."

Her brain was filled with conflicting thoughts, and she struggled to focus on what Max was saying. Max sounded sincere, and he was wearing an earnest expression on his face, but she wasn't moved by his compliments or his effusive praise.

"I owe you an apology for the way I acted in Maui. I never meant to hurt you…"

Jada held up a hand to silence him, but he continued on with his speech. His apology meant nothing to her. She had a strength and confidence she'd never had before, felt as if she'd grown in leaps and bounds over the last few weeks, and she wasn't afraid to tell Max what she thought of him.

"Do you forgive me?"

"No, I don't. I'm done with you."

His jaw dropped, but Jada pretended not to notice the shell-shocked expression on his face. When it came to Max, she was a two-time loser, but from now on she was putting herself first—not him—and if that meant keeping him at arm's length, so be it.

"Jada, you don't mean that. We've been a team for a while, and we have a long history—"

"One minute you want to be with me, and the next you don't. I can't win with you, Max, and I'm sick of trying," she confessed. "I deserve to be with someone who appreciates me, someone who isn't going to run off at the first sign of trouble, and that person isn't you."

"Jada, I screwed up, and I'm sorry." Sighing deeply, he leaned against the hood of his Porsche. "I was scared, and I didn't want history to repeat itself. That's why I pulled away from you in Maui."

"Scared of what? I'd never do anything to hurt you. You know that."

"I've seen relationships that started with promise, passion and love turn to hate all too often, most notably my marriage, and I didn't want it to happen again. Add to that, I have to think about Taylor, and what's best for her, too."

"Relationships are full of ups and downs, but if couples are committed to making things work they'll be successful. I'm not a relationship expert, but my grandparents were happily married for over fifty years, and I plan to imitate their example. Love is hard work, but anything worth having is worth fighting for, and I'm a fighter."

"I believe you." Clasping her hand, Max pulled her to his chest and folded his arm around her waist. "Jada, I'm tired of running. I know what I want and it's you. I'm all in, and if you give me a chance you'll never regret it."

Taken aback by his words, Jada stood silent for several seconds before she spoke.

"Talk about a dramatic turnaround," she said, unable to believe what she was hearing. "Five days ago you didn't want to settle down, and now you're ready to commit. What gives?"

"Jada, you're the right woman for me because you're honest, trustworthy and ridiculously kind. You want the best for me and my daughter, and I love your sincerity…"

Love? The word ricocheted around in her mind, then shot straight to her heart. She couldn't take her eyes off him. Jada was drowning, sinking fast, and there was nothing she would do about it. She was weak for Max, always had been, and there was nowhere else she'd rather be than in his arms. He'd won her over with his gentle caress, his honesty and his boyish smile, and Jada believed he was genuinely sorry about the way he'd treated her in the past.

"That's right, Jada. I love you, and I want to be with you more than anything."

Max nuzzled his face against her cheek, and she giggled as he nibbled her earlobe.

"And I need you to come back to the agency…"

He smelled divine, of expensive cologne and aftershave, and when he licked his lips her mind wandered. His touch was warm, wanted against her skin, and it was hard to concentrate on what he was saying when all Jada wanted to do was kiss him.

"I don't know how much money Shazir offered you, but I'll double it," he vowed. "I won't lose you to him, so I hope that creep is ready for a fight."

Jada hid a smile. There was nothing to think about, nothing to consider. She'd return to Millennium Talent Agency in the New Year and resume working for Max, but she decided to play it cool, didn't want him to know she was overjoyed by his generous, unexpected offer. Not only would she have enough money for her university tuition, she'd be able to help her dad pay off his outstanding credit card bills. "Max, I'm not making any promises, but I think we can work something out. We'll discuss your proposition in the New Year."

"Anything you say, baby." Chuckling, he patted her hips. "I like your new look, but you don't have to get hair extensions or wear revealing clothes for me to notice you. Just be yourself, Jada. That's more than enough."

The smile in her heart spread to her mouth.

"Did you know kissing is good for your health?" Max asked, cupping her chin in his hand. "Studies show it floods the body with endorphins and instantly improves your mood."

Jada arched an eyebrow. "Really? I had no idea. Let's put the theory to the test."

"I was hoping you'd say that." Max crushed his lips to her mouth, slowly and deliberately kissing her as his hands stroked her neck, shoulders and arms.

Sparks flew, and electricity singed her skin.

Cheers and whistles filled the air, and Jada knew they had company in the parking lot. She suspected it was Trey and Derek hooting and hollering like fans at a Lakers game, but Jada didn't care who was watching them. She continued kissing the man she loved, couldn't get enough of his warm, sensuous mouth. They had a lot to discuss— her career, smoothing things over with Taylor, improving his relationship with his ex—but now that they were a couple, Jada was confident they could tackle any challenge, any obstacle, as long as they did it together.

Chapter 19

"It's going to be damn hard for me to keep my hands to myself tonight," Max confessed, a glimmer in his eye and a grin on his mouth. "You look like a sexy Christmas angel, and I'm dying to get you home and *out* of that stunning gown."

Heat flooded Jada's cheeks. Her boyfriend was as handsome as he was charming, and entering the glittering Prescott George grand ballroom on Max's arm made Jada want to pinch herself to prove she wasn't dreaming. He was her dashing ebony prince, and she reveled in his closeness.

"You are the best Christmas gift I have ever been given, and I'm proud to have you on my arm." Max kissed the tip of her nose, then her lips. "*Woman*, I want to ravish you."

Happiness filled her as she snuggled against his chest. They were a new couple, but her heart had always belonged to Max. Her boyfriend was the dictionary definition of a perfect gentleman, and every time he rushed to open a door for her or pulled out her chair, her admiration for him grew. They'd been inseparable since the afternoon they'd left Malibu Elementary School, and now that Jada was returning to Millennium Talent Agency as Max's executive assistant, life was perfect. A dream. Everything she'd ever wanted. "Be patient," she whispered. "Good things come to those who wait, so pump your brakes, Mr. Man."

Max chuckled. "Fine, but don't blame me when I pounce on you later!"

Please do, she thought, her body tingling at the thought of them finally making love. Jada was ready to consummate their relationship, but Max wanted to wait. He said there was no rush since they had the rest of their lives to please each other, and she'd agreed with him. Though once they started kissing it was hard to stop, and if not for Derek knocking on the window of Max's Escalade, they'd still be in the parking lot, making out in his SUV.

"I'm thrilled to welcome everyone to our annual Prescott George Christmas Eve Charity Gala," said the president, waving from the stage. "Tonight isn't just about celebrating with friends and associates. It's about raising funds for a worthy, life-changing cause…"

The über-exclusive event raised hundreds of thousands of dollars for charity every year, and the extravagant silver and gold decorations, esteemed guests, world-class menu and surprise performers made the black-tie party the most coveted ticket in LA. Mingling with city officials, former presidents, television personalities and international superstars, Jada tried not to gawk at the celebrities in attendance. Max loved to socialize with his fellow Prescott George members and their families, while Jada was content in the background, admiring the man she loved.

Gazing down at her outfit, an early Christmas present from Max, she smoothed a hand over her waist and along her hips. She'd fallen in love with the teal off-the-shoulder tuxedo dress the moment she'd tried it on at the Rodeo Drive boutique, and when Taylor declared it was *The One*, Jada had agreed. To complement the dress, she'd styled her hair in an elegant braided bun, added diamond accessories and silver-tone stilettos. When Max picked Jada up at her town house, they'd snapped dozens of pictures and texted them to Taylor, and the tween's witty messages had made them both laugh out loud.

Thinking about the sweet fifth grader filled Jada's heart with love. After the stunt she'd pulled at school, her parents had grounded her for a week, and after several closed-door meetings between mom and dad, things were running more smoothly in the Moore household. Max still hadn't come to terms with the fact that his baby girl wasn't a "baby" anymore, but he was making a concerted effort to be more understanding. The schism between Shay and Max wasn't going to be solved overnight, but Jada was confident their relationship would improve in time. These days, she texted his ex regularly, and planned to have a spa day with Taylor, Shay and her cousins Aubree and Delilah to celebrate Jada's twenty-eighth birthday in February.

Finding table three, they joined the Moore family for cocktails and appetizers. Max introduced Jada to his stepsister, Bianca Duvall, and her blue-eyed date. They discussed the menu for Christmas Day, their plans for New Year's Eve and Prescott George affairs. Jada had fun chatting with Kiara and Alexis about their careers, and when the mom-to-be needed to use the ladies' room and insisted her friends join her, they kissed their boyfriends goodbye and grabbed their clutch bags.

Exiting the ballroom arm in arm, the women giggled and gossiped about the celebrities in attendance. In the lobby, they snapped pictures of the extravagant Christmas decorations, and when Jada's iPhone rang she answered it on the first ring. "Hello! Welcome to the North Pole!" she joked, laughing. "It's Ms. Claus!"

"I wish I could trade places with you," said a female voice with a British accent.

"Hello? Who is this?"

"Someone who envies you. You are *so* lucky to be dating Max Moore…"

Jada held her breath. She wanted to hang up, had a sinking feeling in her chest that the call was bad news, but was curious about what the woman had to say.

"I rented him last Saturday through the Rent-a-Bachelor fund-raiser, and he rocked my world. Literally. Toe-curling sex. Multiple orgasms. All. Night. Long."

A bitter taste filled Jada's mouth.

"Girl, it was the best sex of my life," the stranger purred, her tone one of awe. "You have no idea how lucky you are. Max is an exceptional lover, with a magic tongue, and just thinking about the things he did to me last weekend is making me wet—"

Disgusted, Jada narrowed her gaze. Not wanting to hear another filthy word, she pressed the end button, shoved her cell phone into her clutch purse and slumped against the wall. Glad Alexis and Kiara were in the bathroom and she was alone in the corridor, Jada took a moment to compose herself.

Resting a hand on her chest to slow her raging heartbeat, Jada tried to catch her breath. She wanted to make sense of what had just happened, but couldn't. Her thoughts were muddled, racing in circles, and she couldn't think straight. *Where was I last Saturday? What did I do?* Jada wondered, racking her brain for answers. *More important, where was Max?*

Seconds passed, but when Jada heard "What You Mean to Me," playing in the grand ballroom, she remembered where she had been last Saturday night. Hearing her dad's favorite song reminded Jada how much fun she'd had with her family. They'd eaten too much, drunk too much sparkling apple cider and watched the Christmas-movie marathon on BET. She'd invited Max to join them, but he'd had plans with his brothers, and promised to make it up to her in the New Year. Had he lied to her? Hooked up with someone else last Saturday night? Slept with another woman because Jada was an inexperienced virgin?

"You look like you could use a drink," Christina North, Demetrius's assistant, said, raising her cocktail glass in the air. Jada was glad that Christina was enjoying the party instead of hiding out, given what her former boss had admitted to. "Here, try some of my White Christmas Mojito. It's delicious."

Jada shook her head. "No, thanks. Christina, can I ask you something?"

"Sure, sweetie, anything. What's on your mind?"

"Did a woman rent Max last Saturday through the Rent-a-Bachelor program?"

"Probably. He's our most popular bachelor, and women can't get enough of him…"

Jada felt her eyes tear and her throat close up. She wanted to cover her ears, but she kept her hands at her sides and listened intently to what the brunette had to say.

"Apparently, he plans incredible evenings for his dates *and* gives them their money's worth, if you know what I mean." Giggling, Christina took her iPhone out of her purse, and after several swipes and taps, she fervently nodded her head. "Yup, I checked the logs, and an adult-film star named Nia Pearl paid five thousand dollars for a night with Max. She used her American Express card to pay, and also placed three more bookings for next week."

Christina's cell phone rang, and she excused herself to take the call. Jada was glad to see her go. She needed a moment alone, to process everything she'd just learned about Max. It was hard to believe he'd cheated on her, especially after everything they'd been through, but she'd be a fool to ignore the truth, and had to confront him. Now, before she lost her nerve.

"Sorry we took so long," Kiara said with an apologetic smile. "We were touching up our makeup, and got carried away discussing bridal shows and floral arrangements."

They returned to the ballroom, and the moment Jada saw Max, tension flooded her body. Guests mingled, took pictures and exchanged business cards, and danced to the live jazz band, but the festive, celebratory mood made her feel worse, not better. Max was an esteemed millionaire with celebrity friends, a private jet and gorgeous admirers, and Jada didn't belong in his world. *What was I thinking? Why did I think that we could ever work?*

"There you are." Max slipped an arm around her waist. "You were gone so long I thought you were lost. Baby, let's go. The party's on the dance floor, not over here."

"Who's Nia Pearl?" Jada blurted out, desperate to

get to the bottom of things. "And why did you lie to me about being with your brothers last Saturday?"

His eyes darkened and lines wrinkled his forehead. "Baby, what are you talking about? I didn't lie to you. We took my dad for steak, then watched the UFC fight at the Staples Center."

"Are you hooking up with a woman named Nia Pearl?"

"No, of course not. I'd never cheat on you, Jada. You're everything I need." Max cupped her face in his hands. "I don't know who that is. I've never met her, and I don't want to. All I want is you."

They stared at each other for a long, quiet moment, and her anger slowly dissolved.

"A woman just called my cell, claiming that you hooked up with her last Saturday, and I don't know what to think." But as the words left her mouth, Jada realized it wasn't true. She trusted Max and knew in her heart he didn't do the things the caller said he did. He was her future, the only man she wanted, and Jada believed in him. It didn't matter that they were from two different worlds; he was her soul mate, and she loved him with every fiber of her being.

"Max, I'm sorry," she said, wearing an apologetic smile. "I asked Christina to check the Rent-a-Bachelor logs, and when she confirmed the payment I got jealous. I thought you were cheating on me with another woman, and I freaked out."

His eyes thinned, his nostrils flared, and Jada feared Max was going to lose his temper. It was Christmas Eve, one of her favorite days of the year, and Jada didn't want anything to ruin the Prescott George charity bash. His brothers were slow-dancing with their fiancées, but Jada hoped that if she needed them they'd be able to help her calm Max down. "Baby, it doesn't matter. I believe in you, and that's all that matters."

"What did Christina say?" he roared, speaking through clenched teeth. "Tell me *now.*"

Max balled his hands into fists. He wanted to punch something, to take his frustrations out on the nearest wall, but since he didn't want to scare the other guests he took a deep breath. It didn't help, but when Jada kissed his lips his anger waned. A conversation he'd had with Demetrius weeks earlier played in his thoughts, and a light bulb flashed in his mind. All at once, the pieces of the puzzle fit. Why Christina had lied to Jada about his whereabouts last Saturday. Her unexpected visits to his office in recent weeks. Why his manila folder, filled with damning information about Demetrius, had suddenly gone missing. Why Christina couldn't look him in the eye when they spoke.

Fuming, he struggled to control his temper, the rage boiling up inside him. Searching the ballroom for Christina, he found her standing alone at the bar and decided to put his theory to the test. Waving his brothers over, Max shared his suspicions with his family and agreed with Derek: they had to talk to Christina before the party was over.

"If we don't confront her tonight we might not get another chance," Trey pointed out, speaking in a hushed tone of voice. "Let's do this, bro. It's now or never."

Alexis tucked her purse under her arm. "I'll come, too. Just in case you need backup."

Max took his iPhone out of the pocket of his white tuxedo jacket, found the Recorder app and hit the record button. Careful to conceal his iPhone, he marched across the room and joined Christina at the bar. "I finally figured it out," Max said, keeping his tone calm, even though he was pissed. "Demetrius didn't carry out his sinister plan alone. He needed help, and paid you well to do his dirty work."

Christina made her eyes wide. "I have no clue what you're referring to, and I resent what you're implying. And for your information, I'm a college graduate, not a common criminal."

"Yes, you are. You helped Demetrius frame my father and I want to know why. What did he ever do to you? You don't know him, and you had no right to destroy his reputation."

"I wish I'd done more!" she spit, molding her hands to her hips. "Your family doesn't care who they hurt or how many lives they ruin. I used to have a cushy job and a gorgeous condo in Santa Monica, but now I'm unemployed and it's all *your* fault."

Max stared at her with wide eyes. He couldn't believe he'd ever thought that Christina was a good person, or that he'd considered hiring her to be his administrative assistant after Jada quit. The more Christina badmouthed his family, the more he despised her.

"Why couldn't you leave Demetrius alone?" she asked, her gaze filled with venom. "Your dad screwed his wife and ruined his picture-perfect life. Hasn't he suffered enough? And, now because of your old man, I lost the best job I've ever had."

Derek stepped forward. "This is about money, plain and simple. You ruined my father's reputation, and destroyed the San Diego chapter to earn a few extra bucks. Just admit it."

A sneer curled her glossy lips. "Damn right, I did, and I'd do it again!"

"Good," Trey said, with a nod. "You can tell your

story to the LAPD because we're going to encourage our father to press charges. You need to answer for what you've done."

Christina sucked her teeth. "He's a sick, old man. No one will believe him. It's his word against mine, and I'm an upstanding citizen with a stellar reputation."

"Your *stellar* reputation won't save you this time. I recorded everything you just said." Max raised his cell phone in the air. "If you ever cause trouble for my family, or any of the other Prescott George members, I'll share this recording with the authorities. Understood?"

Wide-eyed, Christina opened then closed her gaping mouth.

Max gestured to the uniformed security guards standing at the ballroom doors. "Christina, you're not welcome here anymore. Please leave, and don't come back."

The guards appeared at Christina's side and took her arm. "Ma'am, come with us."

Security escorted her out, and Christina walked with her head down and her shoulders bent.

"There are my boys. Come over here and have a drink with your old man…"

Max turned around, saw Reginald in his wheelchair and smiled. Frail, but holding on, Reginald wore a tailored suit, burgundy bow tie and a black top hat. Max ordered a round of drinks with the bartender, then handed a champagne flute to everyone in his family. "We can toast to your reinstatement in Prescott George," Max said, raising his glass in the air. "Dad, you're a full ranking member again, with all the rights, privileges and—"

Reginald interrupted him. "But I don't want my membership back. I only came tonight to say thank-you and a final goodbye to my friends in an organization that meant so much to me."

Max didn't get it, and he could tell by the bewildered expressions on his brothers' faces that they didn't understand what Reginald was talking about, either. "You don't want your membership back? Isn't that what this was all about? Why Derek, Trey and I spent the past three months trying to clear your name? So you could be reinstated in Prescott George?"

"No." Reginald's voice was firm. "It was about making peace with my three sons, earning your forgiveness for not being a good father and, most important, bringing you boys together."

Max lobbed an arm each around Derek's and Trey's necks, and his brothers grinned.

"I have my Christmas present, and this holiday season I discovered what matters most in life. Integrity, love and family." Reginald winked. "*And* the love of a good woman! Way to go, sons. You did well!"

Everyone clinked glasses.

Max clasped Jada's hand and gazed deep into her eyes. "Merry Christmas, Beautiful."

Her face lit up. "Merry Christmas, baby."

"Jada, I love you so much it scares me sometimes," he confessed, unable to keep his feelings bottled up inside anymore. "You're irreplaceable, and the only woman I want is you."

"I love you, too, Max. You are the best thing that has ever happened to me, and I want to make more amazing memories with you and Taylor, and this Christmas we will."

Wrapped up in each other's arms, they swayed to the music playing in the ballroom. Max couldn't recall ever being so happy. Life was good. His father was still alive, he had a strong bond with his brothers, a healthier relationship with his daughter, and he had the woman of his dreams. Cupping his face in her hands, Jada kissed his lips, and Max knew in his heart that their love would last a lifetime.

* * * * *

Soulful and sensual romance featuring multicultural characters.

Look for brand-new Kimani stories
in special 2-in-1 volumes starting March 2019.

Available March 5, 2019

LOVE IN SAN FRANCISCO & UNCONDITIONALLY
by Shirley Hailstock and Janice Sims

A TASTE OF PASSION & AMBITIOUS SEDUCTION
by Chloe Blake and Nana Prah

**PLEASURE AT MIDNIGHT & HIS PICK
FOR PASSION**
by Pamela Yaye and Synithia Williams

**BECAUSE YOU LOVE ME & JOURNEY TO
MY HEART**
by Monica Richardson and Terra Little

Get 4 FREE REWARDS!

We'll send you 2 FREE Books
<u>plus</u> 2 FREE Mystery Gifts.

Harlequin® Desire books feature heroes who have it all: wealth, status, incredible good looks... everything but the right woman.

FREE
Value Over
$20

YES! Please send me 2 FREE Harlequin® Desire novels and my 2 FREE gifts (gifts are worth about $10 retail). After receiving them, if I don't wish to receive any more books, I can return the shipping statement marked "cancel." If I don't cancel, I will receive 6 brand-new novels every month and be billed just $4.55 per book in the U.S. or $5.24 per book in Canada. That's a savings of at least 13% off the cover price! It's quite a bargain! Shipping and handling is just 50¢ per book in the U.S. and 75¢ per book in Canada.* I understand that accepting the 2 free books and gifts places me under no obligation to buy anything. I can always return a shipment and cancel at any time. The free books and gifts are mine to keep no matter what I decide.

225/326 HDN GMYU

Name (please print)

Address   Apt. #

City   State/Province   Zip/Postal Code

Mail to the Reader Service:
IN U.S.A.: P.O. Box 1341, Buffalo, NY 14240-8531
IN CANADA: P.O. Box 603, Fort Erie, Ontario L2A 5X3

Want to try 2 free books from another series! Call 1-800-873-8635 or visit www.ReaderService.com.

Once she'd heard the rumor about Singleton Financial
wanting to find another firm to represent their conglomeration,
she'd dived for their information. After being trusted to
work with them—although with Leonardo—within the past
year, she felt obligated to encourage them to stay. What had
happened to make them want to leave? It couldn't have been
the work she and Leonardo had done for them; they'd been
happy customers two months ago.

She wouldn't focus on what else had transpired during
that time, but her skin heated at the memory that was trying

to make its way to the forefront of her mind. Soon she'd be face-to-face with the man she'd been avoiding. They'd never been friends, so it hadn't been that hard to stay away. And yet her body still betrayed her on a daily basis and longed for the boar's touch.

Shaking off the biggest mistake of her life, she zoned in on her career. If she could maintain Singleton Financial as a client, she'd definitely be made partner. No way would she allow the muscle-bound Astacio to snatch the chance away from her.

Once again she wondered why he even worked for the firm. His family possessed more money than Oprah Winfrey and Bill Gates combined. He could've gone to work for his family, started his own law firm or even retired. Jealousy roared to life at how easy his life had been.

A buzz from her phone brought her out of her musings just in time to prepare her for the bear who banged her poor door against the wall before storming in. Their erotic encounter hadn't changed him a bit.

Canting her head, she presented a smile sweet enough for him to develop cavities. "How may I help you, Leonardo?" For a rather uptight law firm, they held an open policy about calling people by their first names, although most of the employees called him Mr. Astacio out of terror. She'd rather scrub toilets at an office building again, a job she'd had in high school.

He stopped in front of her desk and braced his hands on it. "You have something that belongs to me."

A thrill shimmied down her spine at being so close to him. Ignoring the way his baritone voice sounded even huskier than normal, she looked around her shared office, glad to find they were alone so they could fight toe-to-toe. "What's that?"

"Don't play games." He pointed to his chest, about to speak again, when an adorable sneeze slipped out. Followed by four more. So the big bad wolf had a cold. From the gossip mill, she knew he never got sick. Detested doing so.

She got to her feet and walked around her desk to the door. She used it as a fan to air the room out. "Since I can't open the windows, I'd prefer if you didn't share your nasty germs with me."

His clenched, broad jaw didn't scare her. Especially considering how his upturned nose now held a tinge of red after blowing it. The man had a monopoly on sexy with his large dark brown eyes and sharp cheekbones. His tailored suit hugged a muscular body she'd jump hurdles to get reacquainted with if he wasn't such an arrogant ass. *And my competition for financial freedom. Mustn't forget that.*

Leonardo held out his hand. "Hand over the file. It's mine."

She'd worn her favorite suit to work, so she had an extra dose of power on her side. Although her outfit wasn't tailored like his, she'd spent more money on the form-flattering dark plum skirt suit than she had on three of her others combined. Kamilla perched a hand on her hip and hitched her upper body forward in a challenge. "Who says?"

"I do."

Tapping her finger against her chin, she shrugged. "Well, that's all the verification I need. I'll give it to you." She sashayed to her desk and sat on the edge. "Right after I'm finished analyzing it."

Don't miss Ambitious Seduction
by Nana Prah, available March 2019
wherever Harlequin® Kimani Romance™
books and ebooks are sold.

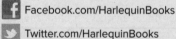